I dedicate this book to my loving wife.

Edward Teach *Better Known as* Blackbeard

JIM LAIRD

authorHOUSE®

AuthorHouse™
1663 Liberty Drive
Bloomington, IN 47403
www.authorhouse.com
Phone: 1 (800) 839-8640

Published by AuthorHouse   03/04/2019

ISBN: 978-1-5246-9651-1 (sc)
ISBN: 978-1-5246-9649-8 (hc)
ISBN: 978-1-5246-9650-4 (e)

Library of Congress Control Number: 2018915050

Print information available on the last page.

CONTENTS

BLACKBEARD

I STAND A IMPRESSIVE 6'4 AND SLIGHT OF BUILD. I HAVE
EYES THAT WILL BORE INTO YOU SOUL. FOR IF YA PICK
A FIGHT I WILL STEAL YOUR SOUL. THEY SAY I AM THE
DEVIL'S SPAWN. THE NIGHT IS WHEN I BRING THE FIGHT.
I HAVE CANNON FUSE LIT IN ME HAIR. THAT WILL GIVE
YOU A SCARE. AROUND ME NECK ME BADLIER CARRIES
SIX PISTOLS. I AM A EXCELLENT SHOT SO DO NOT PLOT. I
WEAR A RED COAT THAT SMELLS OF THE DEAD. AROUND
ME WAIST IS ME SWORD THAT HAS FOUND A MANY HEAD.
DO NOT RAISE YOU SWORD TO ME FOR YOU WILL FIND
THAT YOU ARE DEAD. I HAVE A DAGGER HIDDEN IT IS TRUE
IT MIGHT BE SMALL I BRING TO THE FIGHT IT BE TRUE
TO FIND ITS MARK AND YOU WILL FALL. I HAVE ABOUT
ME WEATHERED FACE A BEARD AS BLACK AS A MOONLESS
NIGHT THE SMELL OF RUM AND SEA ARE APART OF ME.
BE IT KNOWN FOR THOSE TO FEAR SO DO NOT PLEA. FOR
WHEN THEY HEAR, BLACKBEARD TERROR OF THE SEA.

BY JIM LAIRD

PROLOGUE

The inlet was calm, not a stir of a breeze. The full moon lit up the inlet, and a cloud cast an eerie shadow across the water. It was as if Death himself was coming. In the morning, Death would be taking many a soul. A lone ship sat in the inlet with its sails tied tight and no lights lit to give away its position. The deck was ready for battle. Cannonballs were stacked, and buckets of water stood ready to cool the cannons as they spit out their deadly grapeshot. There was a lone light coming from under the door. In the room sat a single figure, the captain. He was deep in thought of the coming battle, wondering whether he would see the sunset the next day. This was no ordinary captain. This was a captain feared by all—Blackbeard. Blackbeard's thoughts wandered, and he began to remember his early days and how his life in piracy had begun.

1

MY STORY BEGINS

I remember it all. The good and the bad. The smells, the sights, the tastes. Even things I wish I could forget. Those—yes, those are some of the strongest memories of all. I sit in solitude on this full-moon night in my cabin. The smell of the sea is crisp in the air. My room is aglow in the light brought forth from a single candle, and I am remembering my earliest of days with Paul, my best friend and confidant. It was a great childhood, for the most part, until the day my life took one of the most crooked turns a life could take.

At the age of twelve, I was already very competitive. I was almost six feet tall by this point and frequently outgrowing the length of my britches. My friend Paul never caught up to my stature and was thankful for my outgrown clothes. We lived on the outskirts of a fishing port. My father was not around anymore. He had been conscripted into service by the British Royal Marines, never to be seen again. So it was just my mother and me. Paul's father wasn't around either. We both helped our mothers with all that we could. My mother made fishing nets, some of the finest in the village. She was able to support us well enough with her talents. Paul and I could always be found together. Thick as thieves we were. On the off times we were not busy around our homes, we could be found fishing in the pond, playing in the fields, and playing chess—our favorite pastime. We played chess often, even though I bested him almost every game.

"Paul, would you hurry up and move? Time is fleeting, and I feel my hair starting to turn gray. Just move something; you know I am going to win," I chided one morning.

Paul moved his knight, putting me into check. Within seconds I moved my bishop and cried out, "Now I have you! Check!"

Paul surveyed the board, moved out of check, and scoffed. I made a quick move and called, "Checkmate!" I jumped around the room, gloating in my easy victory.

My mother called, "Edward, come down to the kitchen. I have an errand for you and Paul."

When we entered the kitchen, mother saw my grin and greeted me with "You've bested Paul at another game, have you?" The look on my face and Paul's said it all. But I still nodded with a devilish grin.

"I need you to go to the harbor and get some fish for dinner. Take Paul with you. Paul, pick up a fish for your mother as well; some fresh fish will do her a world of good."

"Yes, Mrs. Teach, and thank you. She has been taking to bed a bit more as of late," Paul replied. Paul's mother had never been as virile and strong as mine.

We dashed out the door and ran through the yard toward the hard-packed dirt road that wound into town. I slapped Paul on the back and ran past him. "Come on, slowpoke," I teased. Due to my height and long legs, my strides were much longer than Paul's. But I taunted my friend anyway. "I have seen turtles that move faster than you, Paul."

"Show me one, and I will beat it," huffed Paul.

As we arrived at the market, Paul bent to catch his breath, holding his knees. Breathing deeply, I took in the wondrous mixing of smells, both fair and foul, that made up the market. We slowed upon entering the marketplace. We walked a few of the small cobblestoned streets until we arrived at Mr. Chipler's store. mother always said that Mr. and Mrs. Chipler carried the best there was. Since they sold Mother's fishing nets, we were able to carry a line of credit with the store as well.

The bell over the door chimed as we walked in. The scents assailed my senses. I smelled the lavender from the soaps and the tanned leather, but it was the smell of the freshly baked bread that made my stomach begin to churn. The Chiplers sold many wares that came in from the ships in the harbor. Some were quite exotic, like the silks from the Orient and the pearls that were fished from the oyster seabeds. But the one item that always drew my attention was the ten-foot shark mounted on the rear wall of the store.

"Good day, Mrs. Chipler," Paul and I said in unison.

"Good morning, boys; what a pleasure to see you on this fine day," she responded.

Mrs. Chipler was a short, plump, handsome woman. Her graying hair was wrapped in a bun and perfectly coiffed as always. With a sparkle in her eye, she offered us fresh, warm bread that had just slightly cooled. "Okay, boys, I used some flaxseed in this batch; I need some tasters." She broke off two pieces and held them out to us.

While devouring the delicious bread, we nodded that it was wonderful. Not seeing Mr. Chipler in the front of the store, I asked, "Is Mr. Chipler around?"

"No, he has gone to the wharf to buy some fresh fish," she said.

"That is what my mother sent us to market for," I told her. "We will search him out there."

I took one last look at the shark on the wall and got an unsettling feeling in my stomach. We said our goodbyes and dashed out the door toward the pier. The cobblestoned streets were crowded that morning, with horses, buggies, and people going about their daily activities—even more so that day due to the many ships that had docked earlier that morning. The sounds of people in the square selling their wares filled the air. The noonday sun was rising higher in the sky, and the smell of the briny sea was thick in the air.

As we approached the docks, the smells of rotting fish disturbed my nostrils. There were fishermen all along the dock. Piles of fish, eels, and other catches of the day were laid out on tables and in baskets. The fishermen were gutting, cleaning, and scaling their catches. They threw the inedible pieces into the water behind them, feeding whatever might be beneath the brackish water.

Our attention was drawn to a small crowd that had gathered around two of these fishermen. The two fisherman boisterous jabber grew louder. Paul commented to me, "We are never going to find Mr. Chipler in all these people."

"Paul, your problem is that you give up too soon. I will seek him out like a bloodhound," I replied, laughing.

The jabbering became louder as we pushed our way through the crowd that was drawn around two old, seasoned fishermen. They were skilled in the art of cleaning fish swiftly and deftly. They were seated upon two stools at a good-size table, a pile of fish in front of each of them, as well as a bottle of rum between them.

"John, I challenge you to a fish clean-off!"

John, the challenged fisherman, took a swig of rum and set the bottle back on the table. He wore an old leather patch over one eye, and I wondered how he'd lost his eye. The patch gave John a pirate look. I had that uneasy feeling again in my gut, much like the one I'd gotten when I had looked at the shark in the Chiplers' store.

John scoffed and replied, "Charles, I will take that challenge! The usual wager?" He gestured to the bottle of rum.

"Aye." Charles grinned. "But this time I'll be keeping my bottle of rum. Just you wait." Charles was much younger than John. His hair was dark, long, and thick. He wore a worn and sun-bleached tricorne hat. His eyes were bright blue, and he had the beginnings of a beard. As he was much younger, his build was more fit; he would be a fine addition to any quartermaster's crew. Charles stood to take a deep swallow from the bottle. I couldn't help but notice the height of this formidable man of the sea.

Although we knew that we must continue on our search for Mr. Chipler, we were enamored by the scene unfolding in front of us. I, being a competitive young man, was eager to watch the competition. Since Paul was not going to go off on his own, he too was preparing to watch the spectacle unfold.

John said to Charles, "I've told you before that I can catch and clean more fish than you." He took another draught from the bottle.

Charles chided, "All the fish you clean are smaller. We may need to weigh out the flesh in the end."

The competition began.

"I am besting you by four," jeered John.

"Yes, but you are chumming the water with more flesh than scale," scoffed Charles.

I was mesmerized by the speed at which the two men worked. The piles of clean fish continued to rise on either side of the table. The water teemed with life as the men threw the guts and tails behind them. I felt as if my feet were stuck in tar.

The two fishermen continued to work swiftly and deftly. John then stood. His short, stocky build had been made quite muscular from years of pulling anchor. He was no less a force to be reckoned with than Charles. Charles lifted the rum bottle to take a swig, but John snatched it from his lips. Simultaneously John lifted his cutting knife, making sweeping gestures in the air. The crowd laughed. By miscalculation, John slashed too closely to Charles and cut a large eight-inch gash lengthwise down Charles's arm. Though the wound was shallow and not life-threatening, blood began to seep from the cut. I felt a hand on my shoulder. Turning, I looked at Paul, who had gone quite pale. He was holding onto my shoulder for support with one hand, and his other hand was firmly placed over his mouth.

Charles held his wounded arm momentarily and then took another drink of rum. He took his own fish knife and lashed out at John. The blade found a true mark across John's stomach. The women in the crowd screamed, and everyone backed up.

John grabbed his stomach, looking down in horror. His innards were spilling outward between his fingers, and crimson blood flowed freely down his front. He staggered down the dock. Still holding his guts and looking perplexed at Charles, he misjudged the distance between the edge of the dock and the water and fell, right into the jaws of the awaiting sharks. The sharks erupted in a feeding frenzy, making quick work of this unexpected meal.

Mortified by this scene, the crowd had gone silent. A constable burst through the crowd and hit Charles over the head with his billy club. Another constable appeared and put Charles in chains and began to haul him away from the dock. Paul and I cautiously stepped to the edge and saw a shark with an eye patch clasped in its jaws. It looked at me with its evil black eyes, seeming to stare into my soul.

Paul and I made our way through the ever-growing crowd, screaming as we dashed through the streets to my home. I stopped to retch on the side of the road multiple times until bile was all that was drawn forth. I looked back at the scene, still able to hear shrieks. From the hill I could see Charles writhing in his chains, enraged. Then a British Royal stabbed his bayonet into Charles, and the fisherman was still.

Paul reached my home first, but I was fast behind. We burst into the kitchen. Mother was preparing the stew stock for the impending fish. "What's wrong? What's wrong!" she yelled, seeing that we were white as ghosts and trembling.

"Mother, we saw a man gutted like a fish. I think it was only an accident, but then it got worse. His guts splayed forth from his stomach, and he fell into the water and was devoured by sharks! And that's not the worst part," I said, lowering my voice. "The man who cut him was shackled, but then a British Royal bayoneted him." Sobbing and gasping for breath, I stared blankly at the wall.

Mother, knowing me to always be a truthful young man and

knowing the dangers of the wharf, believed me. She sat both Paul and me down and fixed us some chamomile tea to help calm us.

Taking the warm cup into my hands, I whispered aloud in a dead voice, "I will never go near the sea again."

2

A DAY OF SURPRISES

In 1704 I was a strapping young man of eighteen. I was six feet four and lean and muscular. My hair was jet black and hung below my collar. The beginnings of a beard were showing as well.

I was preparing for my last day of school, and my mother was finishing up the breakfast dishes. As she worked, she asked me, "What are your plans after today? You will be finished with your schooling. Do you plan to get a job or try to continue your education in London?"

I gave her a wry smile and said, "I know I don't want to go to sea. I'm actually thinking about joining the local magistrate's office. I have the prospect of an apprenticeship there."

My mother's smile turned into a look of worry, as being a magistrate was very dangerous due to the lawlessness of the community. However, she replied, "You'll need to control your anger. On the bright side you do excel in negotiating and arguing your points clearly."

She then suggested, "Instead of the magistrate's office, how about seeking employment as a barrister instead? You might even be able to get a scholarship to Winchester. You've always been at the top of your class. I do believe Winchester has a fine law studies program."

My mother always wanted better for me. She wanted more than this fishing village for me. She valued education, as my father had. With a small inheritance she had received, she had been able to send me to the nearby school. There was only a little left from the inheritance, but she still wanted to give me the best she could. A scholarship would be a godsend in heightening my education and getting me well on my way to becoming more than what this village could offer me.

"A scholarship to Winchester would be wonderful," I told her. "I could stay with Paul's aunt to keep my expenses low, and I could get a job to help pay my way and even send some back home to you."

There was a knock at the kitchen door. Mother called, "Come in."

"Good morning, Mrs. Teach, Edward," said Paul. Paul had not been as equally blessed as I was in the height department, but he was a stocky, muscular five feet five. His long blond hair was tied back in a ponytail with a black ribbon. He sported a simple mustache on his upper lip. His deep-brown eyes and deep dimples made him very charming to young women.

"Edward and I have been talking about his future," my mother said. "He has decided to pursue a law degree at Winchester. What have you decided to do with your future, Paul?"

"You know, Mrs. Teach, I love horses and would like to become an animal doctor. Winchester is also a fine place to learn medical skills."

"That is very ambitious of you, Paul. I am sure the two of you will both get good scholarships and go far in life." Then hesitantly she added, "Just not too far away."

"Of course not," I reassured, giving her a hug.

I turned and nodded to Paul. "We better get going. We certainly do not want to be late for our last day of school!" And out the door we went.

Our school was small but notable. It looked like a simple colonial home, and in fact it was a former home, transformed into an institute of learning. The front yard was small and gated, and there was a small garden in the back. Students were separated by age groups and learning abilities, so students of varying ages could be within the same room. It was the only school in the area. Only a few families from the surrounding villages sent their children here, not because of the quality of the education but rather due to the cost. Many children worked on their parents' farms or the docks, putting in a hard day's work. Not many families could afford formal education for their children. Many people learned only basic reading and writing skills, enough for them to be able to read the Bible and recite their prayers.

Inside the school there were two rooms on the left of a staircase and two on the right. Each room was outfitted with a blackboard, a potbellied stove, a teacher's desk, and roughly ten student desks. In the two rooms on the left, which were for the lower-level students, each desk had a primer and a hornbook, a paddle-shaped object with the Lord's Prayer on one side and the alphabet on the other. In the corner was a dunce cap. In the two rooms on the right, for the upper-level students, instead of a hornbook, each desk contained a few books of learning, inkwells, and quills. A worn paddle hung by the door along with a hickory switch.

Paul and I entered the first room on the right and took our seats by the window for the last time. These seats were for the oldest and most-educated students. Paul and I as well as a few others had learned in this room for the last three years. I scanned the room, taking in all that the room had offered us during our time here. My eyes couldn't help but land on the paddle and switch, both of which Paul and I had known all too well, all for minor indiscretions. I turned to gaze out the window. I had dreamed off many an hour in this manner, which was partly why the paddle and I had developed such a close relationship.

Our teacher, Miss Frackle, walked into the room. Standing to greet her, we said in unison, "Good morning, Miss Frackle."

"All right, everyone, take your seats. We have only the morning hours before we say farewell to some of our upper-level students. As we all know, there will be four empty seats after the summer holiday. Yes, some will be filled by those ready to move up to this room, but Edward, Paul, Mary Beth, and Richard will be leaving and moving on into the world."

"Good morning, Mary Beth," I whispered. "You are looking exceptionally beautiful this morning."

Mary Beth was five feet four and just over a hundred pounds. She had piercing blue eyes and long ebony hair plaited into a braid. She was the daughter of Lord Galbrith, one of the largest landowners in the county. Her physique showed she was not afraid of hard work. Mary Beth's father, though a lord, made sure all his children learned the meaning of a hard day's work as well as the importance of an education.

"Good morning, Edward," she replied in a strong but whispered voice. "How are you doing this morning of your last day here?" she asked, smiling.

"I am nervous and excited," I said. "Last day here, but first step out into the reality that is beyond this classroom. I have a surprise for you this afternoon, Mary Beth."

"I remember the last surprise you had for me! I fell into Mr. Piddleworth's pond. I am not sure I can handle another surprise from you," she giggled. "So what is your surprise?"

"Now how would it be a surprise if I told you? I can't tell you, but I assure you it will be better than the last one."

A few hours later, young Fondsworth stood up and removed a club from the wall. He went outside and struck the brass bell that hung on the front stoop, signaling the end of the morning's classes. A great cheer erupted throughout the whole school. Some of the students from the upper-level classes went down the porch steps to the walkway below.

Miss Frackle asked Paul and me to stay behind for a moment. Mary Beth joked, "Miss Frackle, will you be needing the paddle from the wall?" Looking at me, Mary Beth said, "I'll be waiting for you outside."

Miss Frackle told us, "You have been my finest students these past three years. Although mischievous at times, you excel at every task put before you. Tell me, what are your plans for the future? Do you plan to go to Winchester or seek local apprenticeships?"

I replied for both of us, "I would really like to study law, and Paul here wants to become an animal doctor. As a matter of fact, we would be honored if you could recommend us for scholarships to Winchester. Paul's aunt lives nearby in London, so our room and board will not be an issue. All we need is enough to cover the courses."

"I was thinking the very same," said Miss Frackle. "The dean at Winchester is a good friend of mine, and I will write to him and highly recommend the two of you."

We both gave Miss Frackle a hug of thanks. "We look forward to hearing from you later," I said, and we exited the building.

Mary Beth was waiting on the bench outside the front gate for me. She saw us coming down the path. "You two in trouble again? And on our last day?" she asked.

I shook my head and grinned. "No, just the opposite this time. Miss Frackle is helping us both get scholarships to Winchester!" I exclaimed.

"Oh, Edward, that's wonderful! I know you and Paul will both get them!"

With a devilish grin, I whispered, "Are you ready for your surprise?"

Mary hesitantly looked at me and said with a sheepish grin, "I guess ..."

"I'll catch up with you later, Edward," Paul said, walking off.

"Yes, come by later and celebrate with us," I called. "Mother is cooking fresh mutton. Bring your mother as well."

"We'll be there!" Paul called back.

I finally told Mary Beth, "I am taking you on a picnic." Just then a carriage pulled up, drawn by a single brown mare. I took Mary Beth's hand in mine, lifted it to my lips, and kissed the back of it. "Your chariot awaits, my dear," I said, placing my hand on the small of her back to guide her to the bench seat.

"Oh, Edward, how wonderful," she said.

On the floor was a basket packed with fresh bread, some cheese, and a bottle of wine. A lone red rose sat on the seat. Mary lifted the rose, inhaling its sweet scent.

As we sat close together on the bench seat, Mr. Miller, the carriage owner, gruffly said, "Push over, lad."

"You're coming with us?" I stammered.

"Of course! Can't leave a young lad and lass unchaperoned." Mr. Miller then let out a loud belly laugh and said, "Here are the reins,

Edward. I expect to have you back here just after sunset. No galloping the horse now. Your father would have my hide if something happened to you, Miss Mary Beth."

I jostled the reins, and off we went. After a while, I pulled the carriage over. Mary Beth surveyed the area. "Edward!" she laughed. "You said this would be a better surprise than last time, but here we are again at Mr. Piddleworth's pond."

I hopped down from the carriage. Mary Beth stretched out and put her hands on my shoulders. I lifted her by the waist and safely deposited her feet on firm ground. Taking the basket in my left hand, I placed my right hand on the small of Mary Beth's back, and we walked away from the pond to the shade of an ancient and mighty oak tree. I spread out the blanket, and Mary Beth sat upon it. "Oh, Edward, this is the perfect spot," she said.

"My queen," I said in a low voice, holding up the bottle of wine, "may I pour for you?"

"Why of course, sir."

I poured the wine into two matching tankards I had purchased specially for the occasion. We broke off some bread to eat and drank our wine, succumbing to the tranquility of the moment.

I leaned in and kissed Mary Beth full on the lips, holding her close. I could taste the wine upon her lips, and the fragrance of her perfume heightened my senses. She snuggled in my arms. "Mary, you are the best. I love you now and forever. I do hope that one day we will marry and spend the rest of our lives on this earth together." I kissed her deeply and passionately.

Mary Beth broke our embrace for a moment and replied, "Oh, Edward, that is my dream as well. I love you too." She returned my kiss with the same amount of passion if not more.

Our hands began to explore each other's bodies. Mary Beth stroked the back of my neck as I pulled her in even closer, caressing her lower back. Our inner passion grew. I kissed her neck, my hand moving to caress her breasts through her dress. She let out a low sigh. I could feel her aroused nipples hardening under her garment. I unbuttoned the top of her dress and slipped my hand in, seeking out her hardened nipples. Taking a nipple between my thumb and forefinger, I gently rolled it back and forth. Her breath quickened, and she unbuttoned my shirt and slid it off my broad shoulders. I made quick work of the rest of her buttons at the top of her dress, releasing her breasts, exposing them to the cool air. Her nipples contracted in response to the air and her growing passion.

I leaned down, and with my tongue I bathed each nipple in turn, her buds hardening even further. With my free hand, I pulled her dress gently up above her knees. I moved my hand softly and slowly up her thigh. Her breathing became more rapid, and her chest began to heave. My hand brushed the material of her undergarment, and I stopped for a moment to kiss her mouth. As I slid my tongue inside her mouth, I tasted some of the wine from before. I touched her passionate flower through her undergarment, feeling the moisture that had arisen there.

Mary Beth reached for my britches and unfastened the buttons. She slid her hand in and pulled my engorged cock free from its constraints. She ran her hands over it. I began to pull her undergarment down, desiring to taste the sweet nectar from her nether lips. Mary Beth grabbed my hand and pulled my face up so she could look into my eyes. "Not now, not here, my Edward. Let us wait till our wedding night, my love."

"Yes, yes. I am sorry. Please forgive me, Mary Beth," I whispered.

"There is nothing to forgive," she replied. "But do let's wait."

We held each other till the sun started to set, Mary Beth's head resting upon my bare chest and my right hand resting upon her bare breast.

3

THE TAVERN

By 1706 Paul and I had accomplished our educational goals, and we had both been offered jobs in our fields. I had an entry-level position at the law offices of Fiddlebaum, Perkstone, and Peck, while Paul would be learning animal husbandry under Dr. Nusbomb, the finest animal doctor in the country. Although our positions were entry level, we would be working for the finest in our perspective fields. We would be moving permanently to London, after a brief hiatus back to Bristol.

"Paul," I said one fine summer day, "we should go to Chauncey's Tavern and celebrate our success."

"I have a better idea," said Paul. "Let's take a sojourn to London before our work begins. We can really light it up there. We can stroll through High Garden and hit many a tavern. Who knows when we will have time to do this once our careers truly commence. I will ask Dr. Biddle to loan us two of his horses. It should only be half a day's ride."

"Sounds like a wonderful idea," I said. "Let's leave tomorrow morning."

We strolled down the road to tell my mother of our great quest. We burst through the door, and I exclaimed, "Mother, we have exciting news to share!"

Mother laughed, "What is it now, you silly young men?"

We explained our plan to go to London. My mother seemed worried. "You boys need to be careful there. You are no longer under the university's protection. The queen's navy henchmen do look for recruits, and you two would be just what they're looking for. Don't forget what happened to your father. He was shanghaied and conscripted into service, and we never saw him again."

Paul reassured her, "Mrs. Teach, we will leave early in the morning, and by horseback we should be there by the dinner hour, well before dark."

"Faster if we run the horses a bit," I said. "We'll stay with Paul's aunt, who lives off Coventry Lane, and we plan to go to the White Horse Inn, which is close by."

"You boys promise me you will be careful, especially late at night in the city."

"See you in the morning, Edward," said Paul. "Good day, Mrs. Teach."

After sunrise the next morning Paul and I lumbered down the path to Dr. Biddle's to inquire about the horses.

"Good morning, Dr. Biddle," Paul said. "Are the horses readied?"

"Good morning, Paul. How is my finest student faring this morning?"

"Very well, thank you."

"Where is it you are taking my horses again?" Dr. Biddle asked.

"We are taking them to London," Paul said. "You know that. Stop kidding me. We are staying with my aunt and will be securing them in her stable."

"This trip of yours does worry me," Dr. Biddle told us. "I know you have been living in London as university students, but now you are mature young men. It can be very dangerous. The queen's henchmen are always looking for a few able-bodied recruits."

Paul reassured Dr. Biddle of our caution, and Dr. Biddle told Paul that the horses would be ready within the hour.

We returned to Dr. Biddle's around nine o'clock and left with plenty of time to make London by early afternoon. Our growing excitement could be noted in our interactions along the route to London. A few times we galloped the horses to further this excitement. We would pick marks and race each other to them. Then disaster struck, and my horse began to limp. We both dismounted. Paul checked the horse's legs and hooves.

To my relief Paul said, "Not to worry. Your horse has simply thrown a shoe. However, this will be a longer trek than expected."

"That means I can still ride him, right? As long as I keep him at a walk and don't run him?" I asked hopefully.

"No, I'm afraid not. You can either hold the reins and walk next to him, or we can double up and tether your horse to mine," said Paul.

"Well, that's a fine thing!"

We walked both horses the rest of the way. When we finally arrived at the city gates, the sun was setting. We walked to Paul's aunt's home to make our appearance.

"We shall return shortly, Aunt," Paul said. "We want to go to the White Horse for a quick ale."

We made our way to the inn. Inside we saw many local men, a few travelers, and some undesirables as well. However, they were all eating and drinking and playing cards with nary a problem. I relaxed a bit. To Paul's pleasant surprise there were also many ladies of the evening about, some prettier than others. Paul looked at me and smiled. We strolled up to the bar.

"Bartender, my good man," Paul said in the deepest voice he could muster.

"What will it be, gentlemen?" the bartender asked.

"Two tankards of ale and two servings of mutton."

The bartender handed over the ale and said, "Find yourselves a seat. The food will be out shortly."

Paul whispered to me, "Have you ever seen so many fine ladies in one place?"

I grinned and said, "You do realize you can have any one of them, don't you?"

Paul's eyebrows went up questioningly.

"Paul, they're all women for hire. Any and all are yours … for a price."

Paul stared at me in disbelief and then smiled broadly.

"Oh no! Not tonight, for the hour grows late and we need to be safely at your aunt's soon," I told Paul. "Let's have one more ale when our mutton arrives and then leave swiftly."

A serving wench brought us our mutton. "Two more ales please, my dear," I said with a smile. We hadn't eaten all day, so we made quick work of the plates. We drained our tankards as well, soon starting on the second round the serving wench brought.

"Let's have just one more ale a piece," I said to Paul when I was nearly done with my second tankard. "Go up to the bar and get them."

"Yes, Captain!" Paul said jokingly.

As Paul was waiting for the refills, I caught him staring at a woman at the bar. She was sturdily built, a little on the heavy side, with pendulous breasts on ample display.

"You like what you see?" she asked Paul. "My name is Maddie, and they can be yours for a price."

"Ye-ye-yes!" stammered Paul.

"Buy me an ale, and you can touch them," Maddie said, teasing him by jiggling her breasts so that her areolas were just peeking out from her top.

"Bartender, an ale for the lady as well," Paul said.

The bartender laughed, "Oh, you mean Maddie here? Lady, ha!" He handed her a tankard. "Here you go, dear 'lady.'"

"You have me at a disadvantage," Maddie said coyly to Paul. "You know my name, but I do not know yours."

"My name is Paul," he replied, taking her hand in his and bringing it up to kiss the back of her hand. "Soon to be Dr. Hawthorne. I am with a friend here this evening. We are celebrating our graduation from Winchester and the beginning of our careers. He is the tall fellow at the table, just there." Paul raised his tankard in my direction. "Why don't you come help us celebrate?"

"I'll bring over my friend Victoria, and we can both celebrate with you," Maddie said.

Maddie called over her friend, a woman of about five and a half feet with alabaster skin, fiery-red hair, and medium breasts straining against her tight bodice.

"Excuse me, sir, are these seats taken?" Paul asked me, trying to be funny.

I was in the midst of finishing my second ale. I looked up at the redhead and almost sprayed my drink over the table. "Yes, do sit down."

"These two ladies would like to celebrate with us. This is Maddie, and this here is Victoria," Paul said.

Maddie made small talk, asking where we were from and where we were staying. All the while her hand was on Paul's upper thigh, creeping upward.

"What are you fine gentlemen celebrating again?" asked Victoria.

"Well," Paul said proudly, "we have finished our schooling. I am now in an apprenticeship for animal husbandry, while Edward here is going to become one of the finest lawyers London has ever seen."

Deepening her hold on Paul's crotch, Maddie suggested another round of ale. Paul tried to carry on more conversation but was clearly feeling very aroused. Maddie slipped her hand down the front of his pants after expertly undoing the buttons with one hand. She felt the moist head of his engorged member. Since they were in a darkened corner, Paul upped the ante and moved his hand up Maddie's dress as well. To his surprise he found no undergarment blocking the entrance to her quim. He instead found a lovely, velvety, slick patch of hair covering her mound. This was Paul's first time with a woman, and he happily explored all he could.

Maddie whispered in his ear, "Paul, I think we would be a lot more comfortable upstairs. I just happen to have a room here."

Paul blushed. "Lead the way, dear", he responded.

I gave Paul a worried look. "It's getting late, Paul. It's almost eleven."

"We won't be long," Maddie said with a wink.

"What happens at eleven?" Victoria asked.

"I hear that is when the henchmen comb the streets looking for strong, young, able-bodied men. They shanghai them, and then the men are never seen again. I know this personally, as my father was taken when I was quite young," I told her.

"Well, there is still time before eleven. Tell me, my knight, what shall we do to pass the time while Paul and Maddie are getting to know each other better?" Victoria asked, firmly pressing her hand on my crotch.

"I shall rescue your thirst and get us another ale," I said.

"No, my knight," Veronica said, "I will get you another drink, but first I must relieve myself."

Veronica left the inn by the back door. I thought nothing of it, as late at night many people relieved themselves outside. She eyed a giant of a man leaning against a post. He was quite burly, with mean-looking eyes, a scruffy beard, and the smell of rum on his breath. He was one of the aforementioned henchmen. "I have two fine subjects for you, Fredrick, but they will cost you fifteen shillings each, not the usual five. One is quite tall, standing well over six feet. The other is shorter and heavyset. Both are quite young and well educated," she said to the man.

"Who are you to barter with me, whore?" Frederick asked, grabbing her throat. "If they are as good as you say they are, I'll give you ten a piece, in addition to a poke."

"Twenty-five total and a poke with both Maddie and me. Final offer!"

"Deal, whore."

When Victoria came back in, she went straight to the bar and got a bottle of rum. "Put it on Fredrick's tab," she said.

The barkeep gave her a knowing nod. "Making money tonight, I see. Shame, they seem to be two fine young men." The barkeep handed her the bottle along with two shot glasses.

Victoria returned to the table and poured two shots of rum. Lifting her shot glass, she toasted, "Here is to you and your new life, Edward. May you have a long and prosperous career." We both took our shots. I coughed, as I had only had ale before. Victoria refilled both our glasses. Again we drank the shots. I gazed at her lips upon the glass, wishing those lips were upon mine. Mary Beth was far from my thoughts at the moment.

With a sultry grin, Victoria stepped back and lifted her foot onto the bench as if to adjust her stocking. But instead she pulled her dress to the side and showed me her fiery-red bush. Looking at me, she lifted my head up by my chin, helping to close my wide-open mouth, and asked, "Like what you see?" She moved closer, her womanly scent intoxicating to my nostrils.

Stammering, I replied, "Oh yes, very much."

After finishing her third shot, Victoria said, "I too have a room upstairs. Shall we finish celebrating upstairs?"

Feeling the effects of the rum, I slurred, "That would be lovely."

As we walked past Maddie's room, Victoria knocked on the door and giggled. I thought she was doing it to tease Maddie and Paul, but later I would realize that it was really a signal that the horrible plan had been set into motion.

Upon entering the room, I was assailed with musty smells and mildew. Victoria sat me on the bed and slowly began to undress. She unhooked her bodice and let it fall to the floor. She lifted her chemise over her head, displaying her magnificent breasts. Her rosy nipples stood erect and hard. Next, she removed her stockings and shoes. Lastly, she pulled her skirt slowly down, stopping for a moment at her pubic line. Then further down the skirt went, past her knees and then to the floor. All I could do was watch. My head and eyelids were heavy from all the hard drink. I rubbed my eyes to clear my vision. Standing in front of me was the most beautiful woman I had ever seen. I scanned her body from her supple breasts to her fiery-red bush. She slowly walked closer to me on the bed. She took my hand and placed it on one of her breasts. She pulled me up to my feet to embrace me. She made quick work of the buttons on my britches and found my waiting erect cock. She knelt down in front of me, sliding my britches over my ass. She told me that my cock was the largest she had ever seen, and she had seen many. She lightly kissed the tip of my cock.

"Edward, get in bed. I have a surprise for you," she said.

"Yes, ma'am," I slurred.

I stretched out on my back upon the bed. Victoria looked at my erect cock, which appeared even larger standing straight up from my body. She climbed across my body, leaned down, and kissed me deeply. She raised her hips and guided my erect cock into her, wondering if she could take my full length. We embraced and fucked for what seemed like hours.

I finally removed myself from her embrace. I handed her ten shillings, double her asking price. I took her chin, lifted her face to mine, and gently kissed her lips. "I do hope to have the pleasure of your company again, Lady Victoria," I said.

Victoria smiled, but there were tears in her eyes, for she knew what was to become of me. I returned to the pub downstairs. Only old men remained, no young men like Paul and me. I spotted Paul at the bar and hurried over.

"Paul, it's really late. We must dash or stay here till the sun rises."

The barkeep overheard our conversation. "Sorry, chaps, I'm closing soon. Time you were on your way."

"What about the henchmen?" Paul asked.

"The British Royals are already at sea," the barkeep said. "They're not hunting tonight, so you are safe."

"Shall we go then?" Paul asked me.

"We shall," I responded.

As Paul and I exited the pub, there was not a soul to be seen on the streets. We did not notice the burly man waiting patiently in the shadows. The man lit his pipe, signaling the other two henchmen in the alley. As Paul and I passed the alley, two henchman ran up behind us, billy clubs in hand. They gave us a swift whack to the back of our heads, driving both of us down to the cobblestones. A few more henchmen arrived with a cart. They succeeded in hoisting Paul and me up onto the cart and took us away to an awaiting ship.

4

THE SHIP

I began to stir, my senses returning to me. My head throbbed. I thought it must have been all the ale and rum I had drunk the previous night. But when I lifted my hand to my head, it came away wet. I peeked through my hooded, heavy eyes and saw that the wetness was blood.

To my dismay I also noticed that the room was moving. All I wanted to do was sleep. Suddenly, as if someone had lit a fire under my ass, my eyes flew open. The room was not just moving; it was pitching. I realized in horror that I was on a ship and had been shanghaied! But by whom? As my senses further awakened, I smelled the foul odors of shit and vomit. I gagged a few times before expelling the previous night's meal onto the wooden planks. I looked around the room and was able to see three other poor souls down here with me. My ears picked up on the sounds of retching and expelling.

My eyes adjusted to the little bit of light shining through the planks from above. I spotted Paul slumped over with a nasty gash on his head as well. *Don't let him be dead,* I thought, and I called out to him. There was no response or movement. I tried to crawl over to him, only to find myself shackled and chained to the floor. There was shouting from above, and Paul began to stir.

"He's alive!" I shouted with relief.

"Mr. Chasten, bring me the bilge rats from below. Let's see what the queen's navy has bought!" someone shouted up above.

"Right away, sir!"

I would learn later that Mr. Chasten hated the job of going down in the hold to retrieve unfortunate men like Paul and myself. However, orders were orders, and he did not want to feel the sting of the whip. He came down the stairs covering his mouth and nose with a kerchief to help fend off the offensive, vile odor that saturated the room. He reached the lock on the chain that secured us men to the floor. He inserted a key and turned it. Nothing happened. He removed the key and took out his knife. With the butt of the knife he struck the lock several times.

"Well now, let's see if ya be opening now," he said. Again he inserted the key and turned it. With a loud crash the heavy chain hit the floor.

He began pulling the chain along the floor and through the shackles, freeing us unfortunate souls.

"All right, ye scallywags, get up those stairs. The quartermaster wants to welcome you aboard Her Majesty's ship the *Black Falcon*."

Slowly we made our way up the stairs and into the bright sunlight. Shielding our eyes from the sun as best we could, we made our way along the deck. Through the sails I caught glimpses of the beautiful bright-blue sky. I thought of Mary and what she might be doing at that moment. How nice it would have been to be with her instead of on this unsteady deck.

"Line up! And be quick about it!" a loud voice bellowed, snapping me out of my reverie and into reality.

"I am the quartermaster of Her Majesty's ship the *Black Falcon*. You have been pressed into Her Majesty's service." Gesturing to a large man standing beside him, the quartermaster continued, "This fellow here, we refer to as Death. Some of you, if not all of you, will find out why that is his chosen name."

Death was a behemoth, easily standing at six and a half feet tall and probably weighing in at 350 pounds. A blue tattoo covered the entirety of one side of his face. Over the other eye was a worn leather eye patch. *I bet whoever took out his eye paid for it with their life,* I thought.

The quartermaster strode to the opposite end of the line from where Paul and I stood. With a polite, painted smile, he asked the unfortunate soul at the end of the line, "What is your name?" The poor soul returned the smile and began to state his name. The quartermaster's smile became a devilish grin as he swiftly punched the man in the stomach. The man bent over in agony and expelled the contents of his stomach onto the ship's deck. Before everyone's eyes, Death grabbed the man, lifted him, and threw him overboard. The process was repeated with the next man.

The quartermaster then approached the third man, who was quite muscular, with a very broad chest. His long blond hair and beard gave him a Viking appearance. In a saccharine voice the quartermaster asked the man his name. The large man tightened his stomach muscles but made no reply. The quartermaster asked him again. Still the man did not reply. The quartermaster struck the man in the abdomen. The man winced but did not bend. Shaking his smarting hand, the quartermaster called out, "We have a queen's man!"

The quartermaster stood in front of me now. I tightened my stomach muscles in preparation for the blow, just as the last man had done. With a friendly smile the quartermaster asked me for my name. I decided to follow the Viking's lead and did not reply. The quartermaster asked me the question again, and again I gave no reply. I prepared myself mentally and physically for the blow, but none was forthcoming. The quartermaster seemed to be finished with me and began moving toward Paul. As soon as I relaxed a bit, though, the quartermaster struck out with snakelike speed, landing his fist deep within the recesses of my gut. I don't know how I managed it, but I winced, drew in a belabored breath, and straightened up. I looked the quartermaster in the eye and replied, "Edward Teach, sir!"

The quartermaster bellowed, "We have a feisty one! Teach will make a fine soldier in Her Majesty's service!" A cheer erupted from the deck.

The quartermaster moved toward Paul. I was very concerned, for I knew that Paul could not handle such a blow as was being delivered. The same scenario played out, and then came the mighty blow. Paul doubled over in agony and began to gag. I yelled out, "No, Paul! Don't vomit!"

It was too late. Death grabbed Paul and dragged him to the side of the ship. Just as Death was about to toss Paul over the side, the lookout hailed from the crow's nest, "Sails! Sails on the horizon! Flying French colors!"

Death looked at Paul, grinned, and set him back down on the deck. The quartermaster yelled, "All men to your stations! We are going to see what those fucking French are made of!"

The deck sprang alive with men moving in all directions. I wondered where all these men had come from so suddenly. A door burst open, and out marched British Royal Marines with bayonets affixed to their muskets. They were ready for battle. Following behind them was the ship's captain. He was dressed in a blue velvet captain's coat with large brass buttons, a large tricorne hat, tan britches, and thigh-high leather boots. He was a magnificent figure of a man. He yelled to the lookout, "Report distance, Mr. Wilson!"

Mr. Wilson shouted down, "I make her about two thousand yards, Captain!"

"Quartermaster?" questioned the captain.

"All is ready, Captain! Preparing cannons as we speak, sir. We will give them a broadside they won't forget!"

"True enough," replied the captain. "Carry on!"

The captain then turned and ordered, "Mr. Chasten, take these three down to the cannon master."

"Right away, Captain!" To us new men Mr. Chasten said, "You heard the captain: move it! Double-time!"

Down the stairs we went. As we approached the door, I heard what sounded like a lot of doors opening and loud rolling sounds. Once I passed through the doorway, the smell of gunpowder assaulted my senses. "Cannon Master Bufford, I have three volunteers!" Mr. Chasten called out.

The cannon master eyed the Viking and me and stated that we were both too tall to work belowdecks. "Take these two back up on deck and introduce them to the rigging master."

Mr. Chasten nodded. "You heard him. Back up you go," Mr. Chasten said loudly.

Paul, however, was perfect for working belowdecks with the cannon master. Being only five feet five inches tall, he easily cleared the five-foot-seven-inch ceiling. When Paul and I spoke later, he told me what had transpired after I was sent topside. Mr. Bufford had met Paul with a smile and said, "Welcome to hell." He then grabbed Paul by the arm and led him down a narrow walkway. "Cannon twelve, here is your new reamer."

There were three men to a cannon. Paul tried to introduce himself but was quickly shut down. "We don't want to know your name," one of the men said. "Life is too short in hell. Here, take this ramrod, stick it in the bucket of water, and after every time we fire, ram it down the barrel. If you don't get the sponge wet enough and there is even one ember left … let's just say you will be leaving this hell at a quicker rate and taking some of us with you."

The cannon master yelled, "Load and roll cannons! Prepare for firing order!"

Meanwhile Mr. Chasten brought the Viking man and me to the mainmast. He yelled to the rigging master, "Come down here, Mr. Grafton! I have two new riggers for you!" I looked high up into the rigging and saw a man who could only be Mr. Grafton.

"Be right down!" shouted Mr. Grafton. Like a spider weaving its way through its web, Mr. Grafton darted down from the rigging and was standing on the deck in mere seconds. As I would learn later, Mr. Grafton had been a rigger most of his time at sea and had become rigging master two years earlier. He knew how valuable seconds were when in the rigging of the ship.

"They're all yours," Mr. Chasten said. "See you after the battle."

But his words fell on deaf ears. Mr. Grafton was already ordering the Viking and me to the second yardarm of the mainmast, the most dangerous spot in the battle. He had no investment in us yet, and this was the best way, he felt, to see whether we were worthy of the challenge. The mainmast was where the enemy, in this case the French, were sure to have their cannons hit first. A broken mainmast would cripple any ship.

"You get to have a great view of the battle from up there," Mr. Grafton told us. "If you see that the battle favors our enemy, the French, you should abandon your posts, climb down to the deck, and help to turn the battle. In the meantime, your job will be to cut the sail loose and let it fall to the deck."

Curious, I asked him, "Why?" I was genuinely intrigued and wanted to know.

Mr. Grafton explained, "The French will be firing at the sails. Some of the chain and grapeshot will be very hot and could set the sail on fire. All you need to do is cut these ropes here." He pointed to the various ropes that would free the sail. "When the sail hits the deck, I already have a bucket brigade at the ready to put out any fires as needed."

The lookout yelled, "Her cannon doors are opening! Closing in on two hundred yards!"

Suddenly, a shot rang out from the French ship. The lookout grabbed his chest and plummeted eighty feet to the deck. He was dead before he hit the deck.

"Turn her to the wind! Open fire!" the captain barked.

The ship turned broadside and let loose a deadly volley. The mast of the French ship exploded. I could hear the men from the other ship screaming. The French then returned fire. I saw what looked to be a hundred flashes. Before I knew it, the mainsail had been torn to shreds, but there were no fires. The cannon fire between the two ships lasted almost twenty minutes. I feared for Paul, who was down below reaming the cannons. Then came a loud explosion that shook the entire ship. Three of our cannons—numbers thirty-three, thirty-four, and thirty-five—took a direct broadside. Body parts lay wasted on the deck below.

Paul left his cannon and the duties therein to try to help some of these unfortunate men. This could be a fatal decision for him, but as he would later tell me, it felt like the only right thing to do. He saw a fellow cannon man holding what was left of his left arm. Paul instinctively pulled off his shirt and wrapped the man's arm. The cannon master saw what Paul was doing and ordered him back to his cannon. The cannons fell silent. The cannon master shouted, "We are being boarded! Get your swords ready! Men, if they come down here, fight for your lives. God save the queen!"

I was still at my position on the mainmast and watched as the French ship closed the gap. I heard the first clangs of many grappling hooks. The captain ordered, "Blunderbuss, port side! Make ready!"

The first of many French marines boarded, and the blunderbuss team made short work of them. The second wave boarded. The Royals made ready for fire, killing most of the French with shot or by bayonet. A third wave of French attacked with much more ferocity. I assumed these men must be battle-hardened marines. The deck was now a slippery sea of crimson. I remained at my post watching the melee below. A mere moment later I found myself falling to the deck below. The yardarm of my post had been taken down by a deck cannon shot. Regaining my senses, I opened my eyes to find myself starting up the muzzle of a French musket. Everything seemed to be moving in slow motion. I watched as the Frenchman's finger pressed against the trigger. A horror appeared in the Frenchman's eyes. His chest exploded open, spewing blood, guts, and entrails all over me. The Frenchman fell dead, covering my torso, his finger still on the trigger.

I looked to see who had saved my life. The big Viking man reached out his hand and helped me to my feet. Our interaction was short-lived, as another Frenchman's bayonet suddenly extruded from my new friend's chest. Blood poured down, soaking me once more. I reached down quickly for a blown-apart musket with the bayonet still attached. Without a single thought or doubt, I ran the French soldier through with the cold, pointed steel. I pulled it back out, and like a cornered animal, I used it to fight and kill as many French soldiers as I could.

My attention was drawn to the helm of the ship, where the captain was sparring, wielding a sword in his right hand. I noticed a French soldier pointing a gun to the captain's back. With catlike agility, I leaped up the stairs, toward the would-be assassin. I took him by surprise and ran him through with my bayonet. A shot rang out. The bullet missed its mark, just grazing the captain, and made its home in a young deckhand instead. The captain turned. Realizing that the shot had been intended for him, the captain acknowledged me with a nod of thanks. We both turned to see the French ship lowering her colors. The British had won the battle. A red flag went up in place of the French flag, meaning they were looking for quarter. Due to this surrender, the British captain was supposed to let the rest of the French soldiers live and not put anyone to the sword. This gesture of raising the red flag was often done in vain, as the British were notorious for not giving quarter. But this day would be different it seemed.

The captains met on the deck of the *Black Falcon*. The French captain had a gaping hole in the left side of his chest and was bleeding profusely.

"You are badly injured, Captain. Do you have a surgeon on board your vessel?" our captain asked.

"He was killed in battle," the French captain replied.

Being gentlemanly, the British captain offered the help of his own surgeon.

"No thank you," the French captain said. "I shall be fine. The day belongs to you, good captain. All I ask is that you let me leave with what Frenchmen are still alive, including the French wounded on board your ship. Those who are mortally wounded, I shall leave with you. One last request: What is your Christian name, Captain? I ask so that when I meet my maker—which now seems likely to happen sooner rather than later—I can ask him to watch over you."

"Jonathan is my God-given name, Captain. Son of Admiral Swinson. Yes, I shall grant all of your requests," the British captain answered. He then asked for the French captain's name in return.

Without further ado the French captain answered while walking away, "Jean Louis Piscoe."

5

PUNISHMENT/ PROMOTION

As the sun began to set, the smell of gunpowder was heavy in the air. An eerie cloud of smoke hung just above the water, like death coming in to claim the dying. Sounds of agony from these poor souls dying of mortal wounds filled the air.

When the captain reached the top stairs to his quarters, he turned and scanned his deck. It looked like a slaughterhouse. The smell was overbearing. Guts and body parts were strewn everywhere. He walked over to the ship's wheelman, who was new. "Good evening, young mate. Where is Mr. Jones?"

"He's down there somewhere," the new wheelman said, pointing to the mass of body parts on the deck.

The captain asked what had happened.

"He took a direct hit from a cannonball."

The captain bowed his head for a second as if saying a prayer. "What be your name?"

"Smith."

"How long have you served in Her Majesty's service?"

"One year, sir."

"Well, Smith, if you would, have the lieutenant come to my quarters."

"I am sorry, sir; he did not make it."

"Who is commanding the British Royal Marines?"

"That would be Corporal John Beckam."

"Would you see that he comes to my quarters then?"

"Yes, sir."

As the captain turned to retire to his quarters, he heard the sounds of men in terrible pain. The task he had for Mr. Beckam would silence those screams.

No sooner did the captain close his door than there was a knock. "Come in!" yelled the captain.

"You wanted to see me, sir?" said Mr. Beckam, who sported a nasty slash on his arm.

"Mr. Beckam, I have a grim task for you."

"Yes, Captain, I already know. It will be dealt with mercifully."

As Mr. Beckam left, the captain wept and said, "God, forgive me for what I've ordered. Please accept their souls. Amen."

Slowly the sounds of screaming ceased.

The next morning was bright and sunny. When the captain emerged from his quarters, the smell of rotting bodies filled the air. He approached Mr. Johnson, the first mate, and asked, "Have you seen the quartermaster?"

"Yes, sir. He went down below to check on the wounded and how many died in the night."

"Please ring the bell and have all crewmen come on deck."

As the bell sounded, the crew began to appear, still bloody from the fight and some injured but in good spirits.

The captain looked the crew over and said, "Men, we are still alive, and I plan to keep it that way. You fought a courageous battle and through your determination we have taken the day. We now have the grim task of cleanup. On a happier note, we have a promotion. Where is Quartermaster Higgins?"

"Here, sir."

"Mr. Higgins, bring that tall crewman forward."

"Aye, sir."

Mr. Higgins took me by the arm and escorted me to the captain.

"What is your name?" the captain asked me.

"I am Edward Teach of Bristol."

"Well, Mr. Teach, I owe you my life. You risked your life to save mine, and any man willing to put his life on the line deserves a promotion. If I am not mistaken, you are one of those poor souls that came on board yesterday. I am sorry for the treatment. You shall find a good home here. I am promoting you to the rank of corporal in the British Royal Marines. I am sorry you will have to wear a uniform that has been spoiled by death, but we will soon have a new one for you. Once again, thank you, Mr. Teach."

The quartermaster yelled to the crew, "Three huzzahs for Mr. Teach!"

After the yelling the ship went silent, as if all the men could tell that something was up and that it would not be good.

The captain looked at the crew. "I am sorry to say we will be putting a man to the sword."

I looked around. *Where is Paul? Was he killed?* A door opened, and two marines emerged holding a man in irons. To my horror it was Paul.

Paul was brought in front of the captain to hear the charge. He was told to kneel and bow his head. I knew deep down why Paul was to kneel, but I did not want to face it.

The quartermaster began, "Mr. Henderson, you have been found—"

Before the quartermaster could read the charge, I spoke up.

Upset, the quartermaster said, "How dare you interrupt! There is room for two here."

"Captain, if I may—" I said.

"Hold ye tongue!" said the quartermaster.

The captain said, "No, let the man who saved my life speak."

"Captain, Mr. Henderson is a friend I have known all my life, and I would like to speak on his behalf and explain what happened."

"Are you saying, Mr. Teach, you want to defend this condemned man?"

"Yes, sir."

"A little out of the ordinary, but I shall allow it. We shall adjourn to my quarters."

In the cramped quarters the first words out of the captain's mouth were "How do you know you can defend this man?"

"Captain, before I was forced into Her Majesty's service, I was going to be a lawyer. I graduated from Winchester, as did my friend Paul—sorry, Mr. Henderson—who was going to be an animal doctor."

The captain looked a little puzzled, for he hadn't been aware of how Paul and I had come on board. "Mr. Henderson stands accused of abandoning his post," the captain said. "You may proceed, Mr. Teach."

"Thank you. During the battle the accused was at his station, I believe as a rammer, one of the most dangerous jobs on the ship. He was on cannon crew twelve. Six cannons down there was an explosion, taking out cannons seventeen and eighteen. Paul—sorry, the accused—left his post to aid and assist the wounded. He was able to save two men. The first man had a badly mangled arm. Using a piece of rope, the accused tied a tourniquet to stop the bleeding. The other man had his leg almost blown off but was alive. The accused finished what the cannonball started and amputated the man's leg. He then found some gunpowder, used it to heat a blade, and applied the blade to the man's leg to cauterize the wound, thus saving the man's life.

"So you see, Captain, my friend saved two men's lives because that is really his duty. If I had not been blown off the yardarm, I could not have saved your life. Just as I had to leave my post to save you, so did Paul have to leave his post to save those two men."

The captain scratched his chin. "Mr. Teach, you have put up a fine defense. These cases usually end in a man losing his life, but in this case I grant life. And let the records show that two men are still alive because of Mr. Henderson. We will grant another promotion. Our ship's doctor was killed several battles ago, and we have not been able to find a replacement—until now."

6

JOHN SMITH

"Quartermaster you may dismiss the crew, but I do not want any of the deck cleaned as of now." As the Captain ascended the stairs, he looked back over the deck. It looked like a human slaughterhouse. The deck was covered with blood and limbs. The Captain had a sickening feeling in his gut. He bowed his head for a moment in prayer and thanked the Lord for the young mate that saved his life and let him see the light of day.

That morning had been one of recovery for his crew. Many lives were lost the previous day and their remains had still been sprawled across the Black Falcon. The Captain spent the morning rearranging his quarters and regaining his composure. A cannon ball had blown through one side of the quarters and blasted a two foot sized hole on the other end. After hours of cleaning his quarters, he stepped out into the afternoon air.

The Captain yelled down to a young crewman "You down there find the Quartermaster and have him report to my quarters with God speed." The young crewmen looked up at the Captain with an "Aye aye sir," and dashed off, nearly slipping to a fall from all the blood.

He found the Quartermaster leaning over Death towards the front of the deck. He had sustained a mortal wound and he knew his time was very short. Death asked the Quartermaster through struggled breaths "Sir ... would you do me one last favor. Can you send up that young mate who's our new surgeon? I know I'm not long for this world, but I want to say something to him.

The Quartermaster acknowledged with a nod, "I shall have him come to you immediately," and rested a supporting hand on death's shoulder. The young crewman reached the Quartermaster telling him of the Captain's request. With that, the Quartermaster said his goodbyes and left for the Captain's quarters.

The Quartermaster knocked on the Captain's door and was greeted with a stern "enter". He walked into the cramped quarters, the roof only several inches taller than he. The Captain was seated at his large desk, sitting upon his throne of a Captain's chair.

"Quartermaster how many are dead and injured."

He replied, "We have seventeen dead, thirty-two injured. Of those thirty-two, eight will probably not see the light of day. I checked on our new surgeon, he is good at what we kept him for," He stated to the Captain with relieved worry in his voice. "Captain, I also have a request from Death."

"Go ahead Quartermaster"

"I regret to inform you he is one of the eight who won't see the sun rise." The Captain's brow furrowed and his disappointment at the statement showed.

"Aye, his time is short. However, he has asked to see the young surgeon for a brief moment."

An eyebrow of the Captain arched at the sudden request. He replied "That is fine. But make haste. I will respect his dying wish, but other men are dying as well and that new surgeon is the only one that might be able to save them."

The Quartermaster stepped outside a moment to task a passing sailor with fetching the surgeon. He entered the low-roofed room once more.

"Quartermaster, who do we have that we may assign the grim task of cleanup and valuables to? What of the new recruits"

"The only two alive of those recruits are the one you promoted and our new surgeon. And the surgeon is on his way to Death as we speak so we can't use him"

The Captain looked to the side and out the window of his cabin in thought, "Tis a disrespect to let a fine sailor like that die without us knowing his name. What was his real name Quartermaster?"

"Not really sure Captain, never found out. I have heard the men yell out now and then 'William'. Maybe that's his name, but we all know him as Death, or John Smith."

"Ah I see. Indeed he has served well. Before you leave to your duties, have the young Mr. Teach report to my quarters immediately."

"Aye aye sir."

"You are dismissed Quartermaster." As he exited the cabin, he glanced back at the Captain through the door who was bowing his head and whispering prayers.

⋯⊰⊱⋯

"Mr. Teach, over here recruit!" The Quartermaser called to me as I was scrubbing the deck alongside the surviving sailors. "Mr. Teach, the Captain has requested your presence. Make haste to his quarters."

"Aye aye Sir. Do I need to be armed, is the Captain in trouble?"
"No Mr. Teach. The Captain just needs to discuss some matters with you of utmost importance."

I ascended the stairs. Like I saw the Captain do earlier, I looked over the deck. The sickening feeling in my stomach that day has never been forgotten. I had never seen so much blood and gore in all my born days.

I knocked on the Captain's door and was welcomed with a, "Enter Mr. Teach."

I stepped inside, the hair on my head grazing the wooden beams of the room, "You wanted to see me sir?"

"Yes Mr. Teach. I want to thank you for saving my life. There is reason people are on board the ship and I think we found yours."

"Thank you sir. I'm glad I could've been there at that moment. I was afraid I was going to be too slow," I said, my body rigid, standing at attention.

"My boy, you had the speed of a cheetah on the hunt. I want to congratulate you on your promotion as well," leaning forward in his chair, **"I** know you will bring a lot to the ship and I know you will move up very quickly."

"Captain I will try to serve you to the best of my ability."

"Now Mr. Teach, I have a very grim task for you but you seem to be very trustworthy. First, may I ask a question, where did you go to school?"

"I went to school in London sir. I studied law.

The Captain replied "And a fine lawyer you would have been. How is it that you came upon the ship?"

"Captain ... you do not know?"

"No I was told that you volunteered, and it now strikes me odd that you would give up such a great career to serve his majesty's British Navy."

"Well ... sir. .. I was shanghaied." I explained to the Captain the circumstances of my last night as a university hopeful. The night Paul and I were seduced and abducted from the tavern.

The Captain was shocked as he heard my story. At the time I wondered if he never knew about the shanghaies his crew committed - if all this time he had been led to believe that everybody volunteered for his ship. It couldn't be.

"Well Mr. Teach. You've come on board just in time. I truly am sorry for what has happened to you. However, I cannot change what the past has done. You are now part of her Majesty's Royal service," he said resolute. He got up from his seat and stood at rest, his hands clasped behind his back. His brow was stern and he looked me in the eyes "Mr.

Teach, The task I have ahead of you for the night is a very grim one. It is frankly one of the worst jobs on the ship.

I remember scratching my head wondering what it could be, what could be worse than living through a battle like I had just witnessed.

The Captain replied "Young man, you will be in charge of the cleanup crew." My face showed the reservations I had.

"But before that can take place, you have to look for all the valuables and store them in my safe here in my quarters.

"I see. Well Captain, I'm sure it can't be that bad."

"Mr. Teach. I assure you, it is *that* bad. I've seen the Quartermaster at work doing this job. It will teach you if your stomach is made of iron or parchment. It is disgusting and gruesome. Although it is a horrid job, I must admit the Quartermaster always seems to take delight in it." He raised an eyebrow in curiosity as he looked up, most likely wondering how anyone could take a liking to the task.

"Alas, you will report to the Quartermaster and he will give you instructions on how it shall be done. You are dismissed Mr. Teach, and good luck. I truly hope you have a strong stomach. I look forward to another talk. It's been very enlightening."

I met with the Quartermaster a moment later. He was already on the deck, surveying the scene, awaiting my arrival. He smiled with a sinister grin.

"What be your Christian name boy?"

"I go by the name Edward Teach."

"Well Mr. Teach, your job is to go around to all the dead and remove all the valuables from their corpses. Their rings, necklaces and even the gold from their teeth. Every bit counts."

I got a sickening feeling in my stomach when he mentioned the teeth.

"Sir, how exactly do I remove the gold from their teeth?"

The Quartermaster took a deep breath, "I'm glad you asked," and lifted an axe that lay against the side of the ship. That sickening feeling worsened as I looked at the axe.

"You will find it shall become very useful, your most useful tool for the task."

I knew this was going to be a job that would make me puke my guts out.

"Mr. Teach. Time for you to grow up," he said as he walked towards the closest body to us.

"This here be a Frenchman. We hate all Frenchman," he raised the Frenchmen's hand by the wrist, his limp, pale hand dangling lifelessly.

"See here Mr. Teach, there are three gold rings on his hand. We will see if the dead will give up without a fight.

I was puzzled at first. *Give up without a fight.* What was that supposed to mean? Once again, there was that feeling **in** my stomach.

The Quartermaster reached down and pulled one ring off. He pulled the second ring off without trouble.

"Ah, I was afraid this might happen. Third ring will not come off," He drew out his blade. With one swift cut, the finger was detached as he removed the third ring from the Frenchmen's bloody finger.

"Now Mr. Teach here comes the worst. We have to see if he has gold in his teeth."

"How are we going to open his mouth?"

He replied with a matter-of-fact grin on his face, "Ya might be tempted to sit there for half an hour prying his mouth open and digging at his teeth boy, but this is how it is done here," He raises the axe high above his head and comes down between the man's teeth he splits his head like a grape fruit. Teeth, blood and brains spill out all over the deck.

"Look here Mr. Teach, a couple of teeth with gold. This'll make the Captain happy," as he reached down holding up the severed top half of the Frenchmen's skull.

"Excuse me Quartermaster."

"Yes Mr. Teach?"

"May I go to the side of the ship for a moment?"

"Get it out of your system boy, for this is now your job."

I sprinted to the edge of the ship, nearly falling overboard as I did. As I was retching, I will never forget the maniacal laughing of the Quartermaster that day. He knew just what I was getting into. He handed me the axe once I regained myself, and walked away. I began the grim task of finding valuables on the dead.

As I scoured the deck for corpses, throwing up half a dozen times already, I came across a very large black mate. It was Death. I walked up to him cautiously. There was a grievous wound on his gut that covered his stomach in blood and was hastily bandaged, most likely by the surgeon who could only do so much before he had to move on. Death looked up and smiled, "I see you made it through your first battle," his hands were weak, unable to even grasp at his wound anymore, his skin had gone pale and sweat was dripping from his brow. Signs of shock or near death as Paul had taught me years ago in a conversation about his medical career.

"I don't think I'll make it through this time. You're going to make a great addition to the ship and the British Royals Mr. Teach I heard you saved our Captain," his breathing was labored and as he smiled, a trickle of blood ran down his chin. "I was telling your friend Paul that I think the battle was a miracle for him. Just as he was going overboard ... we would end up in the fight of our lives. The French frigate saved his life."

I stood next to Death, sorrow for a man I barely knew taking hold, "May I ask your Christian name? I know it's not Death."

"My name huh ... been so long since I used it ... I can barely remember it. White man called me John Smith. I can't remember my other name before slavery."

I asked, "John Smith is there anything I can do for you before you meet your maker. Yes Mr. Teach you can pray for me, for I know the devil will be waiting. John reached out to shake my hand. As he did, blood, shrapnel, and guts spilled out on to the deck. I took his hand as my mind and stomach went numb from the sight. I held on tight to ground myself in the moment as John Smith closed his eyes never to be opened again.

7

SLAUGHTERED GOAT

The sun was setting low on the horizon. The Quartermaster kept a wary eye watching me most of the day between his duties. He yelled out to a young mate, "Bring me a ladle of fresh water."

"Aye aye sir," the young mate proclaimed as he scurried to the barrel of water and back to the Quartermaster, handing him the ladle of water. He made his way to me as the amber, pink, and orange hued clouds of the day set behind him.

"Mr. Teach come over here"

"Yes Quartermaster?" I replied as I wiped my brow.

"You have been doing this task all day long without one break."

"As I told the Captain sir, I will serve this ship to the best of my ability."

"Well Mr. Teach you have definitely proved that with this task," he said with a chuckle as he looked me up and down. I was covered in blood with splotches of brain matter and splinters of bone covering my wrists and thighs.

"Now Mr. Teach, how's that sickening feeling?"

"I don't think I'll have it any more Quartermaster."

He grinned, "Ah very well boy. Here take some water. Your task is almost over. The Captain is going to be very very pleased. Let me see your bucket of valuables," I handed him the bucket I was holding full of jewelry, golden teeth, and assorted coins of French and British value. I had been careful to clean every bit of human remains off of the items I collected. I was even careful to pick up the bucket with a fresh washcloth as not to sully the hands of the Captain once I give it to him. I drunk gulps of water the ladle provided and stood at attention in front of the quartermaster.

"Well well Mr. Teach. You have done outstanding work. Your next duty is to report to the Captain's quarters and hand over the bucket.

"Aye aye sir."

I walked past several mates busy scrubbing and cleaning the deck. I nodded, approving of the job as the deck was almost fully cleaned. I remember realizing how exhausted I was when I walked up the stairs to the Captain's quarters. I knocked on the door twice waiting for the customary "enter Mr. Teach," from the Captain and stepped inside. I always wondered how the Captain knew it was me, but I figured it was one of the reasons he was the Captain and I wasn't.

I opened the door and entered the Captain's quarters, a bit worried of what he would think with my britches covered in blood and my hands lack luster.

"Captain here are the valuables," I said as I handed the bucket over to him. I could see his amazement at the spotless bucket full of cleaned treasure.

"Mr. Teach, most of the time when I assign this task I'm handed a bloodied bucket.

"Well Captain it would not be professional of me to hand my Captain a bloodied bucket. So I took the time to make sure everything was washed and cleaned.

"Well my boy, you have done a fine job. Indeed, you shall be rewarded.

The Captain turned to his cabinet, reached in, and removed a bottle.

"I know this is not normally customary, but you're no ordinary sailor. Would you have a drink with me Mr. Teach?" he took two tankards out and filled them halfway.

"Here's to your health Mr. Teach. May you live long!" he said handing me the tankard. I took it from him and we clanked them against each other making cheers. I thanked the Captain and with one long gulp the liquid disappeared into my stomach.

"Oh my. You be a little thirsty?

"Ahhhh ... Aye Captain, I haven't had much to drink all day."

"Very well then Mr. Teach, I dismiss you. Go get some rest. Tell the Quartermaster to give you as much water as you can drink and a pint of ale."

"Thank you Captain.

"Mr. Teach before you leave, at six bells report back to my quarters."

"Aye, aye." My curiosity had been peaked just that quickly. Surely it must be something important if the Captain requested me that early in the morning.

I left the Captain's quarters with my mind wondering.

I walked up to the Quartermaster who was on the deck overseeing other mates and before I could utter a word, he had already drawn a pint of ale and a pitcher of water.

"Here drink well boy. After you have finished, retreat to your quarters. It has been a long day for you Mr. Teach. Have a nice long rest as well, and at six bells report to the Captain. Oh and be sure to wear your dress coat as well. Godspeed young man."

I retreated to my cot to lay down. Normally I'd spend much time thinking about the day and reviewing what I may have learned. But that night, it was not long before exhaustion and the stress of my task that day took their toll. I closed my eyes and slept deeply.

The next morning I awoke to the sound of the dinging six bells. I slowly crawled out of the cot, my legs and arms sore from the previous day. I dressed in my linens, and remembered to put my dress coat on. I began making my way along the deck towards the Captain's quarters. I reached the top of the stairs and knocked twice.

"Enter Mr. Teach" the Captain, replied.

The Captain was sitting behind his large desk and busy studying charts.

"Have a seat Mr. Teach I have a new task for you," I instantly thought to myself *what sickening task was this going to be.* The Captain stood up and went over to the cabinet again and once again removed a bottle of rum.

"Would you have a drink with me Mr. Teach"

"I would be honored sir."

He poured two tankards of rum and handed one to me. This time I didn't gulp it down, I sipped it. The Captain replied with a laugh, "I see your thirst has been taken care of."

"Yes sir Captain. Thank you so much. And I got the rest I needed. I'm feeling tip-top sir."

"I am glad to hear that, Mr. Teach," he nodded and smiled, satisfied with the achievement. "Now for why I brought you back to my quarters. The task I will be assigning you can be dangerous. However, I believe you are the man for this task."

"Captain whatever task you assign me, I will do to the best of my ability."

"Excellent to hear Mr. Teach. We will be entering the waters off of Port Royal by weeks end. We are low on casks of freshwater. We must replenish soon or we could die of dehydration on the sea. So Mr. Teach your new duty will be to dress in your best attire, pick out 20 men of your choosing, launch a sloop, go into port Royal, and see the Tavern Master at the Slaughtered Goat about purchasing 30 casks of freshwater and 10 casks of rum.

My mind had wondered *why was the Captain requesting me for this.* Of course, as the Captain, his insight was impeccable.

"Why Mr. Teach, indeed you have the uncanny ability of diplomacy and having people think your way. That is a far greater talent than many of the seafaring skills you've learned in the months you've been aboard the ship."

We walked out to the Quartermaster who was busy summoning the crew.

"One note Mr. Teach you might want to get the strongest and biggest crewmembers you can find-those casks are heavy."

I could hear the Quartermaster yelling out to the crew "All right you bunch of scurvy rats! All hands on deck!" The crew gathered quickly, some coming from the Black Falcon's lower decks while the ones on the top deck rushed over to form around the Quartermaster as he paced in front of them.

"All present except for the lookout Captain,' the Quartermaster informed. The Captain addressed the crew "Most of you already know him, but I'm still going to introduce him. This is Lieutenant Edward Teach."

I still remember how baffled I was at the sudden title, "Lieutenant?"

"That's right Mr. Teach you have been promoted to lieutenant. The job you have done cleaning the deck and overseeing the crew and the valuables merits promotion plus how are you going to be able tell crewmembers what to do if you're not an officer."

"Tha ... thank you sir" I said with a strong salute.

The Captain raised his voice again, "Now crew, the reason for this assembly. Mr. Teach here will be choosing 20 crewmembers for his next job. This could be a dangerous mission. Mr. Teach will walk amongst the crew and point you out. This is not a voluntary job. This is an order. Mr. Teach, you have the deck.

"Aye aye Captain. I descended down the stairs to walk amongst the crew. I thought to myself, *Quartermaster was right. It is a scurvy rat looking crew.*

I was slow to make my pick. How could I have known for sure that one of these scoundrels wouldn't just stick a dagger in my back and never return from Port Royal. Searching through all in attendance, I chose the men I had gotten to know to even a little degree. Some I had served with cleaning the deck, other's I witnessed in battle defending the Black Falcon with their lives and fury. I had made my pick and put on my most commanding voice, "Six bells in the morning, meet me here on the deck."

"Aye aye Lieutenant."

"'You are dismissed men. I shall see you when the sun rises."

I had trouble sleeping that night and the next four nights as we sailed to Port Royal. Not only had my cot been moved to a higher quality living quarters closer to the Quartermaster's cabin, but I had been thinking about the mission and if I'd live to tell about it. Would my men live? Would I be a good leader? Before bed that night, Paul had told me all he heard from the crew about Port Royal. How it was a den of pirates and vagabonds - home to miscreants and traitors. Though its wares were exotic and from all corners of the world, the people who retrieved these items were of far less notable quality.

I woke before six bells the day we would go ashore after a night of restless slumber. I went out on the deck and stood at the rail looking out across the sea. I pondered what could occur once ashore. Would I be able to pull this off without being found out as a British Royal? I thought no more on the subject for I knew what would happen if I was to be discovered.

I heard the sound of six bells as footsteps grew behind me on the main deck I walked onto the deck to see the crew of 20 men all saluting me. It was a bump against the ship overlook to the starboard - the sloop loaded and ready.

I commanded, "Alright crew, time to board. We have 5 miles to go."

The crew immediately boarded the sloop in efficient speed, taking positions where needed was last aboard to seem as official as possible.

"Set the sails east by Northeast, set course and let's get underway." I said with the look of determination in my eyes and command in my posture.

The wind did not cooperate whatsoever. In befuddlement, I looked at one of my crewmates. He looked back at me, and with a curious tone, "Lieutenant, have you ever sailed before?"

As embarrassed as a I was, I knew for this mission to be successful, I had to be honest with the crew. "Mate what be your name"

"Charles Wilson sir."

"Mr. Wilson, assemble the crew."

"Aye aye sir."

The crew was spread about the 40 foot long sloop and quickly mustered near the center. I looked them over, and resolving my embarrassment, I told the truth that day on my first mission.

"I'm going to be honest with all of you. I have never sailed, nor have I ever led armed men. However, for our mission to be successful, we have to work together. I'm asking all of you for your help so we may all live through this. Whether I don't return to the ship, if we all go ashore and get caught, or we go back to the ship empty handed, if we fail, death surely awaits us. I don't want that for any of you who I have been made responsible for. You may have only known me a short time, but I assure you, I have no intention of failing you my crew mates"

A moment went by as the 20 men under my leadership stared at me. Smiles adorned some of their faces and nearly in unison, the deck went alive. Crew members scattered to positions along the deck of the sloop. Mr. Wilson, a veteran of the ship began yelling directions to the other members, "Set sails, pull the anchor, set the gaff sail."

A smile etched itself into my face, "Excellent, we are on our way to

Port Royal men." I felt like a new father. I had picked a hell of a crew for my first mission and they were determined and loyal.

"Lookout let me know when you see the port. We will anchor a mile out." I turned to my crew, "This is a simple mission, though it might be dangerous if we are discovered - they will hang us. I will take only 4 men with me on the skiff to keep our presence small." Just then, four very large crewmembers approached

"You can count on us sir."

I looked at the four crewmembers assessing their build and skill. They were mostly my height but far above my weight. They were very muscular at about 275 pounds and wore the leathery skin and scars of seafarers.

"Captain! the port is in sight," the voice of the lookout came from overhead as he clung to the main mast.

"Very well. Start sounding. We don't need to hit a shoal."

The crew member grabbed a knotted rope and began sounding "Aye, aye, we be headin' at about 18 knots." I estimated that we were about a mile off port.

"Lower the skiff. All crew be at the ready." Me and my mates boarded the vessel. The four crewmembers immediately grabbed the oars. As I reached for one, one of the mates stopped me. I was startled and looked at him suspiciously. He quickly replied, "Sir, the Captain does not row."

My inexperience had me flustered once more. "Very well, thank you. Row it be."

As we approached the shore, we could see the rows of houses and stores. Though it was a famous port, it wasn't the largest in the world or anything. But it still held the title of a den of pirates and thieves.

Entering the port there were ships of all sizes. Ranging from the small skiff we had to even larger than the 100 ton Black Falcon

"Row to that dock," I commanded

"Aye aye sir."

As we approached, several men on the dock looked at us cautiously.

I stood up and yelled "I am from the Raven, a very famous privateer ship." One of the men yelled back "Why do you come in by a skiff?"

"You know the King is after the Raven. We do not want to get cornered in the port."

"What do ya be nee din?"

"We are in need of casks of fresh water and barrels of rum."

"Alright. Throw us your rope."

As one of the crewmembers threw the rope to the man on the dock, I lowered my voice and issued commands to my men.

"Men, two of you stay with the boat. I will return shortly." I set out for the tavern with two crew mates behind me.

I was told by the Quartermaster that the tavern master would have the necessary supplies. As I walked along the cobblestone road, I felt uncomfortable in my own skin. The fear of being found out was gnawing at my boot heels. Every grizzled man, promiscuous woman, and dingy child continued to remind me that this was a place I never wanted to be.

After trekking half a mile down the main street, past carriages full of rum and soliciting women, I finally saw the tavern that would satisfy my needs: The Slaughtered Goat. I told my two crew mates to wait outside to keep watch in case anything suspicious went on outside.

When I entered, all eyes were on me-a new face in a new land. I placed my hand on the pistol the Quartermaster had given me early that morning. I walked up to the bar and asked for grog, thinking it would help lighten the tension.

The tavern master looked me up and down. His eyes were like daggers and his face was like stone.

He asked me, 'What be your business here."

"I am from the Raven. We are in need of 30 casks of freshwater and 10 casks of rum for our ship."

"Hmmmm ... is that so? Well boy, you know what I think? I think I smell a rat. I say ye aren't part of the Raven. I think ye are a British Royal. And I can't see a problem gutting ye right here boy," his eyes had the glare of the devil in them, and the possibility of death sunk into my soul. He had caught me and I would be killed in a port with no soul in a thousand miles who would truly care.

Just then, a commanding voice behind me shook me out of my complete fear, "Ahoy Jonathan, give this young man the grog he requested."

"Oh! Yes sir Captain Hornigold."

I had heard this name before in my days on the ship and even before as a young land lubber. He was the famous privateer for the crown that had been known to lead a fiery path across the sea sinking ships of enemy nations and pirates alike. He was standing right next to me, and he had ordered grog, the same as me. His coat was dusted and stained with the life of a sea Captain. As soon as I had acknowledged the presence and reputation of the man behind me in my mind, the tavern had come alive the second his voice pierced the tension. The mates in the tavern knew the Captain was there wanting recruits. The Captain lifted his grog and cheered the tavern.

He looked down at me as he towered above me and asked after a sip of his grog, "What be your name?"

"Edward Teach sir."

The Captain looked at me suspiciously, his hardened face having no need to hide intent.

"What be your ship?"

"The Raven."

"Ahh and how is Captain Fleming?"

"He is very well sir," the lie rung in my head, I had no idea who Captain Flemming was.

"Tavern master, give this young mate rum, and whatever else he needs. His tab is on me!" the tavern master gave a nod of approval and turned to usher some men who worked for him. They ran in back after I reminded the Tavern master again how many casks of freshwater I needed.

The Captain continued, "So Mr. Teach what brings you to Port Royal?"

"We are just in need of fresh water and rum sir."

"Ah, nothing wrong with that my good man" He smiled, and turned his attention to the Tavern master once more, "Jonathan, is Helga still working?"

"Aye, Captain she be in the back finishing up business," he said with a sinister smirk.

"Jonathan, put one on the tab for me. Show this man a good time," He let out a hearty laugh and slapped my back with a show of approval. Jonathan smiled and poured a shot of rum for all three of us.

"Cheers Captain, and smooth sailing to you!" Jonathan said as Hornigold lifted his tankard and gulped it down along with the shot of rum.

"Aye Jonathan! Many thanks," He stood up and slapped me on the back again, "Till we meet again Mr. Teach, smooth sailing," he then leaned over and whispered in my ear, "I know you are a British Royal.

The Raven sunk last week and took all her crew along with it. I saw the wreckage myself."

I could feel the blood drain from my body as my soul shrunk into my heart. The Captain had found me out. He let out a chuckle and spoke low once more.

"Don't worry boy, your secret is safe with me," and exited the Tavern, leaving me at the bar with Jonathan and my shot of rum.

"He be a damn respectable Captain Mr. Teach, pray you get to meet him again someday. Ye will learn more than a lifetime of sailing in one talk with him," as soon as he had finished speaking, out from the back room entered a heavy set woman with breasts bigger than my head. She wasn't the prettiest woman I had ever seen, but I learned that morning at Port Royal that death by drowning in a woman's chest didn't seem so bad.

"Helga, this is Edward," Jonathan spoke with a smile of pride. Helga walked over to me, smiling as she pushed her chest against me smothering the upper half of my torso in her soft plumpness. Before I could muster a word, she yanked my britches down to my knees. The look on my face twisted in embarrassment and confusion as the tavern burst out in laughter. Helga grabbed my cock, bent down, and engulfed it in one motion. She may have had a face I wouldn't brag about seeing, but I can guarantee I had never experienced a pleasure like that until that day. It wasn't long before my knees began to buckle. Her head bouncing forward and backward as I felt embarrassment escape me and sheer pleasure own my body. I had to reach back and support myself on the bar as she continued. Helga finally slowed down and finished me. I collapsed into the bar stool, breathing heavy like I had just set every sail on the ship myself. She stood up and smiled two rows of black teeth. She kissed my dazed body on the lips and walked around to the back of the bar. I pulled up my britches and looked at Jonathan in the most confused face I had ever made.

"Young Mr. Teach, all is arranged. 30 casks of freshwater and 10 barrels of rum are out front and at the ready to transport to your ship. I reached for my pouch of gold that the Captain gave him

"How much ... Jonathan ... do I owe?" I said still recovering my senses.

"Nothing. Captain Hornigold has paid the debt." I finally got my legs back under my body and stood up to begin leaving the tavern in amazement. Just as I took another deep breath, Jonathan handed me one more shot of rum.

"Smooth sailing young Mr. Teach."

"Thank you Jonathan. It has been ... quite the trade," I said as I started my way out of the tavern and outside to meet the men hauling my water and rum. As I made my way down the cobblestone road once more, I stopped for a moment to look back at the tavern. My eyes caught the sign of the building with the letters painted bright red spelling out the *Slaughtered Goat*. I couldn't help but think to myself *I could have been the goat.* I felt the hands of luck guiding my fate that morning. Though I knew I couldn't always count on the helping hand of god to guide me through all of my hardships.

8

QUARTERMASTER

I woke up early as I did every morning. It is my favorite time of the day after all. I exited the lieutenant's cabin and walked over to the rail looking east to watch the sunrise. I have always known how peaceful this time of the morning was. After over half a year of sailing on the

Black Falcon, I had come to love these mornings. When those below deck were still waking, the sea was calm, and the wind was cool with the night air escaping the sunlight at a sprint. Each morning I would ask myself, *what events would* this *new day bring?*

I walked over to the ringing bell and began the morning call. Looking at the timepiece, I wondered how long it would take for my men to assemble in full ranks. "One second, two, three, four," I counted as the men dashed to the main deck, tying and buttoning as they went.

"Excellent time, Very well met mates"

"Well met Lieutenant," they all said in unison.

"Today gentlemen we will be practicing our swordsmanship," I said as I looked among them. For a moment, I glanced below at the lower deck and saw the Quartermaster staggering about. I thought at first that it was just a little bit too much cheer from the night before - until he collapsed on the deck, dropping hard with a thud. Without thinking I leaped over the rail, landed on the lower deck, and ran towards the Quartermaster. I remember the looks of bewilderment on the face of the men as they looked at each other-that leap had to have been at least 15 feet and I landed on my feet.

I reached the Quartermaster as fast as I could and lifted his head. His skin was clammy, and his body was bathed in heat - impossible for such a cool morning. As a swarm of bees, the men gathered around us.

"Hurry pick him up! We need to get him to the surgeon!" I requested. A couple of men put their arms under the Quartermaster's arms and carried him towards Paul's cabin. I ran to the door, pulling it open and yelling, "Paul something is wrong with the Quartermaster!" He emerged rubbing his eyes and trying to gain his senses to understand what was happening. The men carrying the Quartermaster were shortly behind me.

"Quickly, lay him over here," Paul commanded. The men gently rested the Quartermaster on the table while I cleared the papers, tankards, and bags of items off the table. Paul quickly examined the Quartermaster and immediately started thinking of possible answers.

"We must strip him of his clothes we have to break this fever. Bring water and blankets. Soak those blankets in water!" the Captain entered as the men ran out of the room looking for the supplies.

"Paul..." the Captain asked "tell me you know what ails the Quartermaster?"

"Captain, I'm not sure yet. I have some medical journals. I will go through them and see what I can do. I have a suspicion I do not want to disclose at this time till I know for sure."

"Please Mr. Henderson," the Captain replied with sorrow weighing down on his words already, "Do all you can, he is not only the Quartermaster, but my best friend of nearly a decade of seafaring."

With that, the Captain exited the room, his fists clenched and whispering prayer to himself. Worry taking me over, I asked Paul, "Is there anything I can do?"

"Yes Edward, you can pray, just as the Captain is doing."

The men came through the door with what cloth they could find and soak. They handed the wet linens to Paul and he began wrapping the Quartermaster's body.

"Keep bringing me more linens men, I have to break this fever or he won't survive this spell of sickness." Paul walked over to his cabinet reaching and grabbing the medical journals. Thumbing through them as quickly as he could, he was looking for any reference of a fever and the other symptoms he could discern. He threw one down and moved to the other, his fingers moving along the lines of text following his sight.

Until, "There it is! I know what the Quartermaster has. Ague: A sickening illness that is a form of malaria."

As Paul read on, the only cure for this was quinine. Paul rushed out the door, headed straight to the Captain's quarters and banged on the door as he yelled, "Captain I know what's wrong with the Quartermaster!"

The door swung open, "So have you found the cure Mr. Henderson?

"I have Captain"

"Will it save his life?"

"Only if we get it in time."

"What is this miracle cure?"

"Quinine sir,"

"I have heard of this do we have any on board?"

"I'm sorry to report Captain none, it seems at one time we may have had some quinine on board before you became Captain. Captain What is our nearest port" Paul asked

"Oh ... I see ... I am sorry to say the nearest port is three days away."

"That's too long sir. Quartermaster won't last through the night."

'The Captain replied with utter somber in his voice "Mr. Henderson ... He is now in God's hands" and bowed his head. He turned and walked back into his quarters and closed the door.

Paul returned to the infirmary to make the Quartermaster as comfortable as possible knowing he will not make it through the night. Paul sat up all night long wiping the sweat from the Quartermaster, keeping the linens wet. It was all he could do for the man we had followed the past 6 months

At around six bells the next morning, the Quartermaster passed. Paul took the linens and covered the Quartermaster. Paul thought back to when he was first brought on board. This man had held his life in his hands. Now, months later, it would be Paul with the Quartermaster's life in his. A tear ran down Paul's cheek. He had become close friends with the Quartermaster over this time.

Paul found the Captain on the upper deck. "Captain," Paul called out to him "the Quartermaster-" before Paul could finish, the Captain interrupted him.

"I know what you're going to tell me. We shall make burial arrangements. Assemble the crew."

"I'm only a surgeon,"

"Mr. Henderson, you're second ranking till we can find a replacement for the Quartermaster."

"Captain I have an idea. Forgive me for being so bold, but you do need a Quartermaster replacement yes?"

"Yes I do."

"What about Mr. Teach ask Paul?"

"I am ahead of you. I've already thought about that. Let's not concern ourselves with that just yet. Assemble the crew."

Paul walked over to the bell and rang it six times, signaling the time of the Quartermaster's death. The crew assembled on the deck. They knew why they were there.

The Captain stood on the upper deck and spoke to the men, "The Quartermaster passed at six bells. He is now in God's hands. Burial shall be five bells this evening, crew dismissed," As the crowd dispersed, he looked directly at me as I stood merely feet from him, "Mr. Teach I need to see you in my quarters right away."

I arrived at the Captain's quarters, the door was open.

"Captain you wanted to see me"

"Yes Edward come in, these are trying times and sad times."

"Yes Captain we will all miss the Quartermaster he was a fine man," I thought it odd; the Captain never addressed me as Edward.

"I'm in need of a new Quartermaster; I think you are very qualified for this."

71

"Me Captain? I've only served the ship eight months."

"Edward, it might've only been eight months. But what you have learned takes some sailors years to master. Mr. Teach will you honor me, the Black Falcon, and the men, and be my new Quartermaster?

"It would be my honor to serve you and this ship as Quartermaster."

"Well then it is settled. Edward Teach, you are now my new Quartermaster. Let's make this sad moment one of and progress and fortune for the days to come."

The Captain poured two shots of rum and cheered to his new Quartermaster.

"Well Mr. Teach, let's see what the crew has to say," with that, we left the Captain's quarters.

Upon the upper deck, the bell rang. Once again the crew assembled. The Captain yelled to the crew "I have wonderful news Mr. Teach here shall be your new Quartermaster." The crew let out a giant loud cheer.

"Hip hip hurrah! Hip hip hurrah! Hip hip hurrah!"

The crew liked and respected me. After eight months of serving alongside them and leading them on land and at sea, we had grown to cherish the experience we shared and used to continue surviving the many dangers of being in the royal navy.

"Quartermaster, dismiss the crew," the Captain ordered.

"Aye aye Captain," I turned to the crew, "All will assemble at five bells for final farewell to Quartermaster. Crew, you are dismissed."

Paul walked up to me as crew members went their separate ways, "Congratulations Quartermaster. You know, me being the surgeon, I do have some privileges." I looked at Paul questioningly

"Let's celebrate said Paul "I have some rum in my quarters."

"What!" I exclaimed, "Then let's have a shot and celebrate!"

The ship's bell rang five times later that evening and the crew gathered. It was indeed a somber moment. They all looked upon their old Quartermaster wrapped tightly in linens. All were dressed for the occasion. The Captain appeared in full uniform along with me and the rest of the British royals who served the Black Falcon.

The Captain began "God, this was a fine man. Please accept him in your hands for everlasting peace, for he served his majesties fleet with honor and dignity. He will be missed. We now commit the body to the deep for forever lasting peace."

Two men tilted the board the body had been laid upon over and the body slipped into the dark waters never to be seen again.

"Quartermaster Teach," the Captain spoke in a low voice, tainted with sorrow.

"Aye Captain."

"Dismiss the crew."

"Aye Captain," I looked at the crew as the Captain walked back to his quarters "Crew, you are dismissed."

That night I could not sleep. I got up, call it instinct or what have you, but something was bothering me. I opened the door and walked out onto the deck. After nine bells no one is allowed on the deck only the Captain and Quartermaster. I walked up to the rail and looked down at the lower the deck. There was movement. I thought, my eyes were tricking me, but I couldn't take the chance. It was very possible for smaller vessels to sail up to our boat and let pirates sneak aboard. I ran to my quarters and grabbed my blade and pistol.

When I came back out, I slowly crept down the stairs, crouching low and hiding behind the thick wood rails until I could reach the barrels on the deck of the ship. I peered around the barrel to the sight of two men unlashing one of the lifeboats.

"So... "I said as I slowly walked out towards the men, pistol aimed at their head, cutlass at the ready, "It is a little late for a midnight cruise isn't it?"

This startled the men and I could see fear strike their intent, "Oh Mr. Teach, Quartermaster sir, we ... we were just checking the ropes."

"You know the rules mates-after nine bells, no one is allowed on deck. Someone could think you were deserting. Someone could think you were going to steal this boat-"

At that moment, one of the sailors grabbed a marlin spike and rushed towards me. Having practiced the last eight months my skills at gunplay and swordsmanship, I was ready to defend the Black Falcon. My pistol aimed true and I shot, striking the man dead in the chest. Blood spurt from his chest and he clenched his breast as he yelled in agony while falling dead to the ground. I held my blade out and pointed it at the other man.

"Don't be foolish, you don't want to die uselessly like your friend," He dropped the knife he had unsheathed from his belt and raised his arms. The Captain appeared, slamming his door open.

"Quartermaster! What's happening on my ship?" he yelled, pistol in one hand and cutlass in the other. He looked on the deck and saw the dead sailor and the marlin spike still grasped in his hand.

The Captain looked at the other sailor, "Do you want to tell me why you are on the deck after nine bells sailor?"

"Captain I have a lovely wife and two kids. I have served you well for over a year, but there's report of malaria!"

"So," said the Captain "you are going to abandon ship? Or in more formal words, desert?"

"No Captain! I just want to get back to my wife and kids."

"Quartermaster, in the eyes of the British Admiralty, this man is guilty of desertion. We will hold trial seven bells in the morning. Place him under arrest. Two British royals who had come up from below deck with cutlasses drawn came over and slapped irons on the man and took him to the hole.

The next morning at seven bells trial was held for the deserter. All crew was present on deck to witness the event.

The Captain called out, "Quartermaster, you will preside over the trial."

"Aye Captain. Let the trial begin." I turned my attention to the deserter who stood before us.

"You Mr. Wilson have been found guilty of desertion. You know that the penalty for desertion is death. You shall be taken from this world at six bells tomorrow morning. You shall hang by the neck until you are dead. Prepare your soul for what is to come Mr. Wilson."

I could see the sorrow in his face. His eyes had been fixed to the deck of the ship while I spoke. The occasional nod between each of my sentences told me he was listening. But his demeanor was one that had already accepted his fate.

The next morning at six bells, the accused emerged from the hole, irons clamped on his wrists and ankles. I and the Captain were on the upper deck looking down at the accused. Disappointment filled our faces. Shame filled Mr. Wilson's face as he glanced up at the Captain, to me, and then quickly back to the deck of the ship. I spoke low to the Captain, "Sir, I have never hung a man."

"I know it is difficult. But it must be done Quartermaster."

I made eight loops in the rope as I had learned in my months on the ship.

The Captain spoke again after the noose was secured "He shall be dropped from the third yardarm. His neck will snap, killing him swiftly, he will not suffer."

After many months at sea, the sickening feeling had returned to my stomach. But the sentence had to be carried out.

I gulped down my hesitation and commanded, "Take the accused to the third yardarm men," crewmen drug his body up the ropes and positioned him on the yardarm. One remained to hold him against the mast to prevent him from jumping to his death and avoiding proper execution. I climbed up the ropes to the yardarm to meet them, which I had done many a times before, but never for something like this. I put the noose around his neck and spoke some of the last words he would ever hear, "Mr. Wilson, may God receive you. I know you're a good man and you only want to go to your family. But desertion is desertion. You will hang by the neck until you are dead.

I took the rope in my hand, feeling the weight of this man's soul.

"Are there any last requests. Do you have anything to say Mr. Wilson?"

"No Quartermaster."

"So it shall be," I put my hand on his back, and pushed him off of the yardarm. His body fell nearly 15 feet before I heard the rope go taught. But something was wrong; I heard the guttural sounds of his body struggling for air. The rope I had tied around his neck came loose near the top of the noose and got caught up in the rigging. The condemned man suffered immensely. He struggled as his eyes began bulging out of his head. His lungs were looking for that last breath the rope would not allow. I drew my pistol to put the man out of his misery and pointed it directly at his head

"Quartermaster! Put that pistol away. The sentencing is hung till death!" The Captain commanded.

I could feel Mr. Wilson's soul struggling to fix the noose, but it was simply too weak to change what had been done. His head turned pink and his eyes filled with blood. He kicked and groaned out cries of pain through a broken airway.

After an excruciating minute of me and the crew watching him struggle to death, the body stopped twitching. The tongue, covered in blood as he was biting it in utter and complete pain, fell to the side of his mouth which was hanging open. Shit and piss filled his pants and started to drip onto the deck below him. He was dead. I quickly took my blade and cut the rope that was holding him up. The body hit the deck like a heavy wet sack of potatoes, landing in his waste and blood.

"Take the body and throw it overboard men," I said with disgust and shame now filling my face, "You there, get some water to wash off this man's waste."

"Aye sir," they all said in unison. Crewmembers grabbed the corpse and walked to the side of the ship to toss the body overboard. Under us awaited a gang of sharks who had been drawn by chum poured over before the hanging. I walked over and peered down at the sharks as they feasted on the corpse of Mr. Wilson. My own self disappointment took over and I drew my pistol. I fired it at the largest shark I could see on the surface, striking it between the eyes and killing it instantly. I put my pistol away and turned to walk away. The Captain was already behind me with an expression of stern sorrow, "Let this be a lesson Quartermaster. Always make sure your drop is clear. Before the man you respected has to suffer even more pain and shame," he walked away, up the stairs, and into his quarters.

"Crew, you are dismissed," I commanded as I walked up the stairs and to the Quartermaster's quarters. I took off my pistol belt, laid down my sabre, and wiped my hands in the tub of water I had in my room. I sat on my cot in exhaustion, I wiped the sweat from my brow and thought to myself, *what an eventful day.*

9

HOME

It had been 10 months since that fateful day the quartermaster passed and the deserter fled the same night. We had sailed hundreds of miles. We had several dozen new members join the Black Falcon and I had filled out the role of Quartermaster. The Captain had trust in me and I had trust in the Captain. Paul had become a fantastic surgeon and excellent doctor. He kept us alive through all four seasons and the many hazards each could bring. Our lives on the sea had grown on us and we were accustomed to the many obstacles life in the British Royals brings.

One morning, the Captain walked to his door and yelled down to me.

"Quartermaster, I'd like to see you in my quarters"

"Aye aye Captain on the way." I reached the Captain's quarters and walked over to him as he stood at his desk staring at the sea charts.

"Have a seat Mr. Teach. I have something to discuss with only you,"

"Only me Captain?"

"Yes with you. It will be our decision alone Qartermaster. We are going home back to London," A cold sweat swept over my body. This is where it all began. It had been so long since I had been to or thought of London, that I was unprepared for the prospect of actually returning.

"Aye Captain. What can I assist you with?"

"Well Quartermaster, I am plotting a course. I have two options to choose. One course would take us a year and a half to reach London. However, it is safe of any naval threats. The other option is a course that would get us to London in less than six months..."

"But why is that not the obvious choice Captain?"

"Mr. Teach look at the sea map," he pointed to an area he had drawn on, "you see that red triangular area?"

"Yes Captain."

"That is French patrolled waters, and the 6 month course would have us spend at least 2 weeks in those waters."

"I see Captain."

"Not only that Quartermaster, I hear they have 300 ton Man-o-wars with two 18 pound cannons each. Just one of the ships would make short work of our hundred ton ship. Although those ships are powerful, our ship is fast and we would possibly be able to outrun any ship that could pose that type of threat. I'm asking you Quartermaster, what say you?"

"Captain ... I'm up for a battle if need be, and I know this crew can handle anything the French would throw at the Black Falcon. Also Captain, the men have been wanting to get home for some time now."

"Then it is decided. We take the short route. Quartermaster, assembled the crew."

"Aye aye Captain."

I walked out the Captain's quarters and rang the bell three times the crew assembled down on the main deck. The Captain stepped out of his quarters and walked to the rail to address the crew.

"I have good news men. We are going home to London. The ship is in need of repairs to keep it afloat and functioning properly, and I think we are all in need of repairs ourselves. For some of you this might be the last time we will sail together. When we reach port some will retire. Some will go back to their families. Some may never see London."

The crew looked confused at the comment. One crewman piped up, "Captain may I ask, what do ye mean we may not see London?"

"I shall answer that men. We are going through French patrolled waters. It is the fastest way to get to London, thought we will have to spend at least 2 weeks sailing through waters they have been known to patrol. It is dangerous, but I believe we will be able to make it through."

The crews' faces were concerned at first, but the prospect of home delighted them. The crew yelled, "Hip hip hurrah! Hip hip hurrah! Hip hip hurrah!"

The Captain looked at me, "We have our answer set the course Quartermaster, were going home."

The morale was high on the ship that day. The men were happy.

It had been a while since we heard the crew sing while a working. The Black Falcon set sail for London.

***

Three months passed since course was set. We were now approaching French waters. I yelled up to the lookout, "keep a sharp eye out. We are now in French waters."

The reply came back "aye Quartermaster I will keep eyes like a hawk."

We had sailed for twelve days in French territory without meeting a single ship of French origin. Many of the sailors gave praise to lady luck and the Gods of the sea. We continued on our daily tasks, trainings, and lookouts. The Captain and I continuously kept our guard up, ready for anything to occur.

On the thirteenth day, our luck had met its match. The lookout yelled down to us "two ships, starboard, sixty cannons at least, out too far to tell where they hail from.

I yelled up, "Keep an eye out on them."

I ran up the stairs to the Captain's quarter's and knocked furiously on his door. The Captain opened the door and the look of concern on my face had set the tone in seconds.

"Begging the Captain's pardon, we sighted two ships."

"Mr. Teach can you tell what type of ships"

"No Captain they are too far."

"Get my eyepiece. Let's see what we're up against." As the Captain looked through his eyepiece his blood ran cold and his breath became shallow

"Oh my God. Those are the largest ships I have ever seen. God help us," he dropped the eyepiece to the deck. I picked it up and peered through. The ships had already begun a maneuver by the time I looked.

One was moving port side and the other was moving to our starboard while heading directly at us. The one starboard broke out, most likely to flank us, while the one portside kept a straight course.

I yelled, "All men to battle stations. Cannons at the ready! Muskets loaded! We're going to have a battle! God save us all!"

Paul came up from the infirmary and asked, "What's all the commotion?"

"See for yourself," I said as I handed the eyepiece to him. Paul looked through the eyepiece for a moment. He slowly put the eyepiece down and looked at me.

"Are we going to win this battle Edward?"

With a concerned look I replied, "I don't know if we will"

There was a large puff of smoke from the port ship. All eyes looked towards the huge ball of iron that was hurtling towards the ship. An enormous crash and thundering blow struck the ship mid center putting a tremendous hole in the deck. No one had ever seen a hole this large.

"Stand at the ready men!" I commanded.

The Captain yelled out, "Quartermaster, go down to the infirmary. See if the Surgeon needs anything!"

"aye Captain," I ran to the infirmary as fast as I could. Slamming the door open, I asked, "Paul, is there anything you need? More bandages? More hands? Hell, a shot of rum?"

Paul looked up from his patient who had a giant wood splinter protruding from his hand, "The rum sounds damn nice. But while you're here, you can do me one favor. Over at the cabinet, grab some bandages for me please."

"Yes sir." I stepped off to go towards the cabinet when suddenly the whole ship shuddered. I was knocked to the deck, hitting my head on the cabinet and cutting my forehead. For an instant, I was confused as

I fought to regain my senses. I Stood up and shook my head to control my sight which was wavering in and out. I looked around, wondering what happened. I looked to where I was just standing next to Paul and his patient. Paul and the patient were not there. I looked around the room and saw that there was a large gaping hole in the side of the ship. It showed the path of the cannonball's travel as there was another smaller hole on the opposite side of the ship. There was no table. There was only blood, guts, bone and hair.

"Oh my God. No! What happened to Paul? Please. No. You can't be dead, please," My mind was shaken, my heart was broken, and my soul was crumbling. I had just been talking to my closest childhood friend, and but a moment later, his existence disappeared into the abyss of the sea. I turned to look out the large gaping hole in the wall. It was the other French ship that broke formation earlier; she has arrived to the battle.

"Curse you Frenchmen. CURSE YOU! I will kill every one of you for this!" I heard chains hitting the deck above. They were boarding to try and take us with minimal effort. I realized that only the main guns from earlier and one volley from the sister ship had been made. They must have assumed that it was all they would have needed to disable our ship and break our morale. They were wrong. In a fury, I pulled out the cutlass on my hip and ran up the steps to the main deck. Opening the door, I came face to face with a Frenchman pointing his musket at my chest. I could see the fear and surprise in his eyes. That hesitation was all my rage needed to give me the initiative. Before I could think the action, my body responded and thrust my blade forward piercing the man's heart killing him instantly. I pulled the sword from his body fiercely, blood sprayed out and covered his shirt and pants in his life fluid. His body fell onto the steps below me and I quickly vaulted over it. I stepped out onto the deck and steeled myself.

Carnage was everywhere as Frenchmen poured onto the deck of

our ship. I looked to my right and saw one of my fellow crewmen dead on the ground. In his cold hand he was grasping a French cutlass. I removed it from his body with my free hand and held up both my swords above my head,

"Men of the Black Falcon, CHARGE! His Majesty's eye is upon us this day!" that rallying cry brought the fury of our crew upon the Frenchmen who dared assail us.

Standing in my way, a Frenchman had a sword at the ready. The rage of Neptune took me that day. I confronted him head on.

Lifting the Cutlass high in the air yelled, "From hell I came, into hell I will send your soul," and I brought down the blade hard and fast. His guard had wavered after my battle cry and my sword plunged down into his being. The blade split his skull in two. It continued down to his sternum as I heard the crack of ribs while the blade sliced through them. His torso split down the middle in two from the top of his skull down to his balls. His body hit the floor and his organs spilled out onto the deck. What seemed like gallons of blood drenched the area around his mutilated corpse.

The battle aboard the Black Falcon seemed to halt for that moment as all eyes fixed on me. The red of rage filled my eyes and blood covered a majority of my body. The souls of our assailants clung to me, but would find no solace. I lifted the Cutlass still dripping of the blood and guts from the poor Frenchman and went on to slay half a dozen more Frenchmen as my men defended our vessel. I decapitated one man with a strong slice. I cut both arms off of another who attempted to flank me. I fell another Frenchmen with a kick to his gut and thrust through his rib cage, piercing lungs and spraying blood on to his countrymen behind him.

"Hold the line men. They will know the savage men of the Black Falcon this day!"

"Huzzah!" the men of the BLACK FALCON let out a strong battle cry as they fought hard for their lives and knew this was the defining moment of our ship. If we faltered here, we would all meet the depths of the ocean. As I cut down the men in my path, my eyes caught those of the French Captain. Anger like no other swelled within me at the sight of the man who began the assault. I pointed my cutlass at the French Captain across the expanse between our two ships and yelled with the power of a hundred men "From hell I came, into hell I will send your soul!"

Fear filled the French Captain eyes. He grabbed the shoulder of what looked to be his Quartermaster and spoke to him with the soul of cowardice in his face.

He clenched his teeth and raised his blade in the air, "Que! est ce diable? Battre en retraite! II y a un Diable! Battre en retraite!" The French aboard the Black Faicon lowered their guard and immediately attempted a retreat. They ran to board their ship and pull from the battle. As they escaped, I cut down two more who would never set foot on a French ship again and pistols from our crew unloaded into several attempting to cross the boarding planks.

I quickly looked around the deck to assess the situation. It looked like the deck had been painted red. I came up to the Captain who I could see standing on the upper deck. The Captain was breathing hard and in shock that the Frenchmen were retreating.

"In all my days, I've never seen a man split in half. One hell of a fight Quartermaster," he told me.

"Quartermaster, we need to get the injured down to the infirmary. Time for Paul to earn his money," hearing the name of my friend who died an unjust death, I fell to a knee, passion engulfed me and my words wavered between attempting not to sob in front of the Captain

"I'm ... sorry to report Captain ... we have no ship surgeon anymore. When I was downstairs, a cannonball... smashed into the Black Falcon. It blew a whole straight through to the other side and took the surgeon with it. There was nothing left of him ... "I looked up at the Captain as tears streamed down my face.

"I do swear this Captain. I will kill every Frenchman; starting with that French Captain."

Now thinking back to that day, what happened next was a blur in my own memory. But from what the Captain told me, some form of demonic strength took over me. Wiping my face and accepting my anger, I stood up, walked to the bow of the ship, and reached down to grab a French musket. I tried to fire it at the French Captain, but it wasn't loaded. In rage, I let out a yell of instinctual fury, and with the strength of 10 men I broke the bayonet off of the musket and threw the blade at their ship. I remember yelling across to their ship as the blade sailed through the air, "from hell I came, to hell I send your soul!"

The Captain told me he swore that the French ship must have been 50 yards away, though the bayonet flew through the air as if some evil hand grabbed the blade and guided it towards their deck. In the wildest of possibilities, it struck the French Captain in the back, skewering him through the chest. As he looked down, the point of the bayonet protruded from his breast and he fell dead to the deck.

Stuck in my violent frenzy, I had also thrown the musket itself right after the bayonet. It landed squarely on the back deck of the French ship and the hand of the devil was at play once more. The second it hit the deck, a Frenchmen nearby was startled, tripped and fell to the ground, and the musket he held discharging its deadly ball killing the wheelman.

I looked back to the Captain, his mouth open and eyes wide in amazement, "Captain, let's finish what we started," I turned to the deck where the surviving men of the ship had been standing, watching the hand of a devil guide my rage.

"Load all cannons men, they have no wheelman and no Captain! They will not be ready for a fight after running with their tail between their legs!" the men started scurrying around the ship and half ran to the cannon deck. "Fire all cannons at will!

Grapeshot, chain shot, and ball all blasted with the continuous explosive thud of cannons from the lower decks. Through the air, lead poured onto the ship that stole the life of Paul. Chain shot hit the main mast, shattering it and disabling their mobility. Grape shot peppered the ship, shredding the sails and mutilating the godforsaken French crew. All the while, cannon fire blasted away at their hull.

Seeing vulnerability in their ship, I ran down below to the cannons. I went behind a couple crew members who were in the process of loading the cannon. I went into action, pulling the cannon back-an act that usually takes a couple men to do with effort, poured the powder in, loaded the ball, and rolled it back forward into the port. Peering out the Canon port, I aimed the Canon at an opening in the ship a volley had made earlier. By my determination, I believed it could be the powder keg of their ship. Smiling a sick smile of gruesome satisfaction, I hollered "From hell I came in to hell I send all your souls!" I fired into the ship.

The ball went right through the hole, hitting deep in the bowels of the ship. After but a second, a bright flash and enormous plume of fire and smoke erupted from the innards of the ship. I hit the powder keg and the ship exploded in a glorious sound and sight. The deck blew outwards sending bodies flying in every direction, cutting the ship in half and sending thousands of pieces of wood sailing into the air. Limbs joined the shrapnel as Frenchmen were incinerated along with a large part of the ship. We had bested a ship nearly three times our size, and the other ships sailed away.

I walked back to the top deck as those in the cannon deck stared at my ascent. Those above deck stopped and fixed their gaze on me. I was covered in the blood, gore, and souls of our enemy and my face had a smile fixed across it at the victory we had seized. There was fear in the eyes of my men. But as I strode closer to them and dropped my blades on the deck, a wave of relief washed the utter dread and sorrow from their beings. Though they were taken aback by the rage that consumed me, I had saved their lives.

"Crew, we live to fight another day. This day we have taken victory and we will be sailing home to London." A cheer of survival reached out from the guts of every member of the crew who survived the ordeal.

That day reminded me of the very first day I spent on the Black Falcon. As I ascended the stairs to my quarters, I looked at the deck that was painted in the fluid of dozens of men. Body parts everywhere had been sprawled across the wood and blood began soaking in the many fabrics and cloths on the deck. It looked like a slaughterhouse.

As the Captain walked on to his quarters, he let out a loud command to those below, "Men, we have survived, but now is the grim task of cleanup. Time for the sharks to eat."

While I walked to my room, my head tilted down and as the Captain had done all those months ago, I began a prayer. But it was not a prayer to God, for he had no part in the tragic deeds that unfolded this day. That day, I had prayed to the devil himself, thanking him for giving me the fury necessary to slaughter the men that took the life of my closest ally and dozens of other crewmen. Only the Devil would answer the calls of men who did battle in such savage way.

As the days wore on and London grew closer, I remember becoming more distant from the humanity of the crew. At night the crew would hear me chanting my prayers, and in the mornings, their eyes would have a slight tinge of fear as they listened to my commands. They were saying that no man on earth could have done the things I had done in that battle. No man could have done it without the help of the devil himself.

One night, on our path to London, a crewman came to my quarters, "Captain needs to see you right away Quartermaster"

I reached his door and knocked, "Come on in Quartermaster,"

"Hello Captain, you wanted to see me?"

"Would you like a shot of rum?"

"No Captain"

"Edward, you've never refused a shot of rum with me?"

"If it be so, then I shall have a shot of rum Captain."

"Excellent to hear," he poured me a shot and handed it to me.

"Cheers to returning back to London."

We lifted our glasses and drank heartedly.

"Edward, I am truly sorry about your friend. He will receive all honors for his service aboard this ship. His family will be taken care of. When we reach London there is a wonderful tavern I must visit for a task. I would like you to join me there. I have great news for you.

"I look forward to it Captain, thank you."

"Land ho!" comes from the lookout above us. Months after that fateful day, and a full two years and several months after being coscripted into his Majesty's Navy we had finally reached our home. All eyes looked to the west and on the far horizon, the buildings of London began to peer over the edge of the sea. We made it.

"Drop sails, tie them tight, prepare to drop anchor men! We are home," I commanded as I paced the ship, ensuring all duties were accounted for.

The rowboats were let down the sides of the ship and launched. The men are excited to finally be home after two years of sailing, fighting, and nearly dying on the expanse of the sea. They're going to go and see their families and rejoice in time away from the horrors of battle and survival. I can't help but think of fellow crewmen who aren't able to enjoy this time.

The Captain walked up to me, "the tavern's name is the White Horse." "The White Horse Sir?" that's where it all began. It was where I was stolen. Would I see Victoria? What would I do if I did? Slit her throat or hug her for the man I've become? My thought was interrupted by the Captain, "I'll see you there."

I jumped into a rowboat and headed towards the docks. Approaching the docks, a crewmember who was rowing for me threw the line to one of the dockmen. They tied the boat to the dock and I stepped out of the boat and onto London for the first time in years.

Several crewmembers surrounded me and thanked me for saving their lives. They wished me well on my travels. After the goodbyes and farewells, I travelled up the cobblestone street towards the White Horse. My hand was on the hilt of my sword keeping it at the ready. I feared no one, and I was prepared to meet the people who set me on the path I have lived the past two years.

Upon entering the White Horse, the Captain was seated to the right. Two tankards sat in front of him. The Captain motioned for me to come over.

"Be there in just a moment Captain," I walked up to the bar it was the same barkeep from that night. Nothing about his face, hair, size, or scent changed.

"Why do you look at me so?" asked the barkeep.

"Death" I replied.

The barkeep looked oddly at me, "I don't understand Sir ... death?" at that moment I drew my British heavy dragoon pistol and pointed it directly at the barkeeps head.

"You remember me?" I asked, the fire of hatred spewing from behind my teeth,

"N .. no sir. No I don't," he cried out as his eyes widened in complete fear.

"Let me refresh your memory then. Two years ago, there were two young men fresh out of college who came in here to celebrate graduation. Those two young naïve men met some ladies of the evening. They seduced them, keeping them late into the night. They begged to stay in the tavem till morning because they knew the dangers of wondering around at night. You chose to tell them no. You see, these two young men had their whole lives ahead of them. One was going to be a lawyer and the other a doctor, but their lives were broken in an instant."

A cold sweat broke out on the barkeep's brow. He was shaking in his boots and his hands were clinched hard on the bar in front of him.

"Sir ... I. .. I don't know what you're talking about."

"Oh yes you do. I am one of those young men who begged that night to stay here. You lied to us, and you sold our lives away without a single second of remorse or regret."

I cocked my pistol and my brow twisted into a killer instinct. A whimper left the barkeeps throat and he began pissing himself in fear. Retribution looked him dead in the eyes and he knew that his soul would be condemned.

I remember thinking to myself how much I wanted to send lead barreling through his skull and out the other side. But he wasn't worth the effort. He wasn't worth getting arrested and hung by the local authorities.

"You are a pathetic little man, never let me see the filth of your face looking in my direction, or I won't let you live to see another day," I put my gun back in its holster and walked over to the Captain.

"Well Edward, I see being at sea has made your heart, mind, body, and soul hardened. Keep those traits Quartermaster, they will guide you through the life you will live," I took a seat at the table with the Captain and he slid me a tankard of ale.

"The reason I brought you here is because you have served me well, the Black Falcon well, and you served the crew well. Your time with her Majesty's Navy has come to an end Mr. Teach," He cheered my tankard with his, took a swig and continued, "However, your time at sea is nowhere near its end. You will have a new Captain," my eyes widened and my mind raced. I was never prepared to hear that I would work with another Captain.

Again, the Captain's skill at insight was unflawed. "Don't worry Edward; I'm sure it will be an experience like no other for you. In truth, he is standing right behind you," My soul was flustered and my heart started to beat fast. I had no idea what awaited me once I turned, though I knew it would be the start to a new era of my life. My head turned around and up and my eyes locked with the man who stood but three feet behind me.

"Nice to meet you again Mr. Teach, I am Captain Hornigold, and you are going to be my new Quartermaster."

To be continued

Follow Edward in the next book called "Blackbeard: No Quarter Given". Watch as Edward becomes the most famous and feared Pirate to sail the seas: Blackbeard.

AUTHOR BIOGRAPHY

I have been portraying Edward Teach (Blackbeard) in various contexts for over seventeen years and have played that role on stage for fifteen years. Blackbeard actually was six feet four inches, and that is my height. As part of my costume, I wear five pistols and sometimes a blunderbuss and a sword. All the guns are real, and the getup weighs about sixty pounds in total. I do kids' pirate shows, and I also do historical talks about Blackbeard. My fellow pirates suggested I write a book, and *Edward Teach, Better Known as Blackbeard* is the result.

Printed in the United States
By Bookmasters